'I feel attrac  **declared.**

'It's a bit sudden, [...] shock.

'Sudden but possible, wouldn't you say?' he replied, and a husky undertone in his voice etched its way along Christa's nerves. She knew, without a doubt, that he was deliberately seducing her, projecting his appeal to entangle all her senses in his potent sexuality.

And her body was falling for it!

Having pursued many careers—from school-teaching to pig farming—with varying degrees of success and plenty of enjoyment, **Meredith Webber** seized on the arrival of a computer in her house as an excuse to turn to what had always been a secret urge—writing. As she had more doctors and nurses in the family than any other professional people, the medical romance seemed the way to go! Meredith lives on the Gold Coast of Queensland, with her husband and teenage son.

Recent titles by the same author:

WINGS OF CARE
WINGS OF PASSION
WINGS OF DUTY
COURTING DR GROVES
PRACTICE IN THE CLOUDS
FLIGHT INTO LOVE

WINGS OF SPIRIT

BY
MEREDITH WEBBER

MILLS & BOON®

*First published in Great Britain 1997
Harlequin Mills & Boon Limited,
Eton House, 18-24 Paradise Road, Richmond, Surrey TW9 1SR*

© Meredith Webber 1997

ISBN 0 263 80190 X

*Set in Times 10 on 11½ pt. by
Rowland Phototypesetting Limited
Bury St Edmunds, Suffolk*

03-9706-49599-D

*Printed and bound in Great Britain
by Mackays of Chatham PLC, Chatham*

CHAPTER ONE

'YOU'RE always getting dressed to go to other people's weddings!'

Christa gritted her teeth, sucked in her breath and tugged at the zip on the floaty, silk-chiffon creation she had been nagged into buying during yesterday's shopping expedition with her mother.

'It's three years since I've been to a wedding, Mum,' she argued. 'I hardly think that qualifies as "always"!'

'And that one should have been yours!' her mother wailed. 'Daniel and you instead of Daniel and that English girl no one knew. It hasn't lasted, you know! He's already running around town with someone else—'

The zip finally slid home, and Christa turned to face her mother.

'I'm leaving here in five minutes,' she warned. 'We do not have time for a re-enactment of Daniel's wedding or an update on his sexual conquests. Not that I need one, as you've managed to bring him into every conversation we've had since you arrived.'

She smiled at her mother to soften the impact of her forceful tones, then dropped a kiss on the top of her head and continued firmly, 'Put on your hat, check you've got your airline ticket and walk out to the car—or you'll have to take a taxi to the airport.'

Her mother, cut off in full flow, did little more than nod and move across to the bed to pick up her hat, but as she left the room she turned back to face her daughter.

'It wouldn't have happened if you'd married him like

5

we arranged,' she announced, then hunched her shoulders to emphasise her disapproval and walked away.

'Wouldn't it?' Christa muttered to herself, infuriated by her mother's habit of always having the last word. 'And as for their even considering an arranged marriage! In this day and age!'

She cast a fleeting glance at herself in the mirror, and grimaced. The dark-haired, dark-eyed woman in the fashionable party dress looked OK—even attractive—but it was her mother's image of her youngest daughter reflected there—a person with whom Christa had always felt ill at ease.

'And as for Daniel not playing around after marrying me!' She continued her soliloquy as she shoved a handkerchief and small hairbrush into the handbag her mother had bought to go with the dress. 'The only reason he pretended to go along with the stupid "arrangement" in the first place was because he realised he couldn't get me into bed any other way. Fancy there being a girl in Darwin he hadn't bedded.'

'I beg your pardon?'

Christa stopped short, aware for the first time that she'd been delivering her furious denunciations aloud as she raced through the little cottage, shutting windows and locking doors.

'I was thinking about work,' she said quickly to her mother, and hurried her to the car before she could question the statement.

Family messages and unwanted motherly strictures occupied them on the short drive to the airport and it was with relief that Christa finally ushered her mother through the security gates and into the departure lounge, where she joined the queue of people filing out to board the flight.

Christa pressed her nose against the glass, determined

not to leave until she had seen her too-loving relative climb the steps into the aircraft which would carry her home to Darwin.

'Won't you be late for the wedding?'

She turned slowly, reluctant to lose sight of the small, upright figure marching across the tarmac. The clear, crisp voice had to belong to Andrew Walsh, the nominal health worker and driving force at the settlement of Caltura.

'What are you doing here?' she asked, but her attention wavered and, before he could reply, she turned back to peer through the glass wall.

He didn't reply but moved closer, looking out towards the plane.

'Are you waiting for someone who's due in?'

He raised a hand to rest it against the barrier and, in her peripheral vision, she glimpsed his long, tanned fingers and the scattering of black curling hair on his wrist.

'I'm waiting for someone to go,' she explained, refusing to be distracted from her mission by silky wrist hair. 'See that small woman in the bright blue hat—well, that's my mother. One of my recurring nightmares is that she might decide, at the last minute, to come back—to stay longer than her allotted three days.'

'You don't like your mother?' he asked, his beautiful voice deepening with disapproval.

Christa watched the blue-hatted figure reach the top step, turn and wave towards the building. She lifted her own hand in reply, although she knew that her mother couldn't see her.

'I love my mother,' she said huskily, turning to face Andrew with a silly rush of emotion dampening her eyes, 'but I can only take so much mother-daughter stuff at a time.' She drew a deep, calming breath. 'I mean, look at this dress.'

She stepped back, held the skirt out with her fingers and twirled around in front of him.

'Does all this floral chiffon look like the sort of clothes I'd buy? Can you imagine me going into a shop and actually paying good money for such a thing? I'll wear it once a year if I'm lucky, and won't ever feel comfortable in it.'

Irritation chased away the sentiment that had threatened to take hold.

'I think it's charming,' he said gravely, startling her so much that she looked up into his face to see if he was teasing her. 'And you look very lovely in it,' he added, shocking her even more.

'Well, it's not me,' she said gruffly, embarrassed by such a personal observation from a colleague she both liked and admired. Searching for a diversion, she studied him more closely and realised, for the first time, that he was dressed in 'city clothes' in place of the moleskins and faded blue bush shirts he usually favoured.

'And what are you doing in town?' she asked, hoping that her quick appraisal of this new-look Andrew hadn't been noticed. He looked stunning, and she'd probably stared—once her anxiety over her mother's departure had diminished enough to let her think of anything else!

'I'm here for meetings with Jack at the Base on Monday. When Peter heard I was expected he suggested I come for the weekend and join in the wedding celebrations.'

'Oh!'

Christa felt her usual easy flow of conversation dry up. For some months now Andrew Walsh's lean and darkly handsome face had been sneaking into her occasional day-dreams, but the dusty, abrupt, always-in-a-hurry Andrew she knew at Caltura was far less devastating than this riveting male in tailored black trousers and a grey, raw-silk, knitted polo shirt that clung to his shoulders and draped across his deep chest like a lover.

She sneaked another look at him, and found his grey eyes studying her intently—as if he, too, was reassessing the person he had known.

'And we're both going to be late,' he added, his wide mouth stretching into a smile that caused a tiny flutter of excitement in her heart.

'Do you want a lift?'

She blurted out the words, while the weirdest thoughts jostled for brain-space in her head. He's OK for day-dreams, a voice said—for fantasy stuff—but this is a man who's way out of your league.

'That would be great,' he replied, the almost musical notes of his voice interrupting her internal monologue. 'I was going to take a taxi. Do you mind waiting while I collect my luggage from the carousel?'

Christa nodded, but she frowned as she watched him walk away. Luggage from the carousel? If he'd flown in from Caltura on a light plane he'd have his luggage with him—and he wouldn't have come in to Rainbow Bay through this interstate terminal. Light aircraft taxied to the other side of the airport—over by the Royal Flying Doctor Service hangar.

Where had he been? Back to wherever he'd come from? More questions than answers—that was always the way with Andrew Walsh. Even at Caltura an aura of mystery hung around him. Mystery and money!

She saw his tall figure bend and straighten again as he lifted a battered leather case from the moving belt. Then he was walking towards her, a tall, dark-haired man with an athletic stride which typified the boundless energy he seemed to possess. She fixed the image in her mind—freeze-framed for an instant—seeing him as the symbolic traveller passing on his solitary journey through life—this

stranger the aboriginal people of Caltura called 'The Man
from Yesterday'.

'OK?' he said as he reached her side again. She set aside
the foolish conceit and led the way out of the terminal.

'Where have you been?'

The question popped out of her mouth without much
forethought, but she consoled herself that it was a normal
'airport-type' question.

He didn't answer immediately and she glanced sideways, catching a sudden gleam of white teeth behind his
smiling lips.

'Very refreshing, the direct question,' he told her, the
smile widening until it crinkled up the tanned skin at the
corner of his eyes. 'I'm so used to the roundabout way
the people at Caltura seek out information that it comes
as quite a shock to be asked outright.'

The remote-controlled doors slid open at their approach,
and they walked out into bright sunshine and warm air
that wrapped around them like a knitted shawl.

'Not that it did much good,' she muttered, wondering
if he had any intention of answering her question—or was
all his praise of it a way of fobbing her off? 'The car's
this way.'

She crossed the road, assuming that he would follow.
Maybe he liked the 'mystery' tag! Or maybe there was
something more sinister in his evasiveness.

'I've been in Melbourne,' he told her as she opened
the trunk and then stood aside so that he could lift his
suitcase into it.

'Oh!' she said again, uneasily aware that her customary,
easy-going friendship with Andrew, developed slowly
over months of regular work together and evenings talking
in the community hall or walking in the moonlight after
dinner, had vanished. Today she felt as if she was trying

to make conversation with a stranger.

She studied him for a moment. His head was bent as he shut the boot with gentle pressure and his profile— high forehead, well-shaped nose, wide, unsmiling mouth and firm chin—gave nothing away. A very private man, this Andrew Walsh, she reminded herself.

'I'll unlock your door from inside.' She slipped away from him to open the driver's door, then reached across and lifted the catch to let him in.

He folded himself into the seat, seeming to absorb all the air in the little coupé as well as taking up more than his share of the room.

Knowing that they were already running late, she tried to banish her distracting thoughts and concentrate on getting to the wedding. Her fingers fumbled the keys into the ignition and, after three tries, her normally reliable little car finally started.

Her passenger made no comment about her ineptitude, or the car or even the weather. He sat, his knees tucked up towards his body, and stared out at the road.

'Sorry it's such a squeeze,' she apologised as the silence between them grated against her nerves. 'You know Peter, Allysha and Nick, of course,' she added, naming the RFDS flight staff who had visited Caltura. 'Have you met Katie?'

'She was at the Stampede,' Andrew reminded her but his voice seemed to come from far away, as if his astral body had remained somewhere else—possibly Melbourne—and had not yet caught up with his physical presence.

'It's a great day for it.' Christa ploughed on valiantly. Any conversation was better than none, and if he wasn't going to introduce the weather as a topic there was no reason why she shouldn't. 'And the Stones' garden should be perfect at this time of the year.'

Why am I doing this? she wondered as she heard her voice echo back at her in the close confines of the car. And why should I feel uneasy with Andrew?

She slanted another look sideways, but he was peering out of the window as if he were a tourist visiting Rainbow Bay for the first time. He must have had his hair cut while he was away, for there was a strip of paler skin between the short-cropped black hair and the tan that began lower down his neck.

The tiny interval of paleness gave him an impression of vulnerability, but when she looked again he had turned towards her and the gleaming grey eyes were those of a decision-maker—a man of action. Andrew Walsh was a man in charge of his own destiny—a man to whom 'vulnerability' would be unthinkable!

'Is your family a close one?' he asked, and she felt her mind shift a few mental gears. The weather had obviously held no appeal as a conversational topic, but she could handle the change.

'Extremely,' she said drily. 'To the extent that I'm regarded as a total renegade for, a, not being married by the time I was twenty-one, b, having a career and, c, leaving—not only the family home, but also the town where I was born—Darwin.' Keeping her eyes on the road, she held out one hand and shrugged dramatically as she rolled her eyes in mock despair. 'Can you imagine the scandal?'

'Bad, eh?'

'Bad?' she echoed. 'We're Greek-Australian, my family! You must have heard of Greek tragedy?'

She looked quickly at him but didn't wait for a reply.

'Well, it was played out at my house for weeks—until every last dramatic nuance had been drained from it and

everyone was so exhausted I think they were glad to see
the last of me!'

Andrew chuckled, a rich, mellifluous noise that rumbled
up from somewhere near his toes and rang like tiny bells
down Christa's spine.

'I get the picture!' he said. 'And did you decide to give
marriage a miss because you were set on a career?'

How many times had she evaded that question?

She steered the car carefully into—and out of—the
roundabout, turning it towards the Stones' house, before
she looked across at him. His face showed nothing more
than polite interest, and she was goaded into the truth.

'I grew up understanding—knowing, somehow—that I
would marry Daniel, the son of my parents' closest friends.
When I decided I couldn't go through with it a career
seemed the best way out of the ensuing uproar—especially
a career that might eventually get me out of town and
away from the tearful recriminations that I knew would
go on for months.'

She glanced at him again and added with a rueful grin,
'So, you see, I'm a dedicated nurse, motivated not by high
ideals but by a desire to live somewhere far removed from
the people I love most dearly.'

'Arranged marriages are part of Aboriginal custom,'
Andrew said quietly as Christa braked and drove more
slowly, searching for a parking spot among the cars that
lined the usually quiet street.

'I hadn't ever heard it was that organised,' she
responded, only half following the conversation as she
swung the car around to try the other side of the street.

'Well, maybe it isn't,' Andrew agreed, 'but in the old
culture there were definite family lines within which
people could marry. Ritual beatings have occurred in

relatively recent times when a girl went off with someone not of her "skin".'

' "Skin"?' she queried, backing competently into a small space in front of Jack's big silver Range Rover.

'It's the word used for a related group within the tribe,' Andrew elaborated. 'People were expected to marry within their tribe, but not within their own family or clan. Common sense, really, if you consider the implications of intermarrying within families.'

Maybe his astral body was in Caltura, not Melbourne, Christa thought, reaching down to pull on the high-heeled sandals she'd slipped off while she was driving.

'So, to that extent, the marriages are arranged,' he finished.

'Great,' she told him, glancing up from her task with a smile twitching at her lips. 'I could have married one of Daniel's seven brothers instead of him! What a field of opportunity that would have provided.'

'Not much joy in any of them?' he asked sympathetically, his eyes gleaming like wet slate.

'None at all!' she said emphatically, straightening up and pulling the keys out of the ignition. 'Every one of them thinks he's the ultimate gift to women. Talk about big-headed. Just because their father owns half the fishing fleet, and has made millions packing and freezing seafood for export, they believe they're special. Honestly,' she continued, warming to the subject and looking into his face as she appealed for his understanding, 'a girl would be better off with a nice, home-loving mass-murderer than one of the Eliskas.'

'And Christa Eliska would sound dreadful anyway,' he finished for her, his watchful gaze twinkling down at her in such a way that she felt her bones begin to melt.

'How right you are!' she responded, hoping that the

gaiety in her voice didn't sound forced—or false! This situation was ridiculous! It must be a hangover from some ancient mating urge that was causing her body to respond to Andrew's. Maybe her mother's visit, or the wedding atmosphere, had dredged it up from somewhere in her subconscious psyche.

Andrew extricated himself from the car and she paused for a moment, settling her nerves, before she, too, climbed out. He waited on the footpath, then took her arm as they walked through the gate into Eddie and Susan Stone's lovely garden.

As the sounds of laughter and high, excited conversation floated towards them Christa realised the implications of arriving at this double wedding not only late but with Andrew holding her arm.

She pulled away from him, and he stopped and looked down at her.

'Are you OK?'

She tried a smile to ward off her embarrassment.

'I'm fine,' she said, 'but I'm imagining what all the staff are going to think when we walk in together. Susan Stone is a great nurse and a wonderful woman, but gossip is the breath of life to her and within a matter of minutes she'll be planning another RFDS wedding.'

She saw a strange glint in Andrew's eyes, then he smiled and winked at her.

'I could wait outside and make my entrance a little later,' he offered, 'but I doubt anyone would fall for that. Or we could try the truth—we met by accident at the airport and you kindly offered me a lift.'

He made it sound so trivial that Christa felt embarrassed she'd mentioned it.

'Of course we can,' she agreed, and turned towards the

noise again. 'Not that anyone will believe it!' she finished
gloomily.

She led the way around the side of the house, then
paused again to take in the fairy-tale setting.

White water lilies floated on the surface of the swimming pool, transforming it into a floral carpet. In between
them small white candles burned, sending spirals of an
aromatic fragrance into the air. The paved barbeque area
had been transformed into a bridal bower, with tall spikes
of ginger flowers thrust into white pots and white ribbons
tied into the green tropical shrubbery.

Christa caught the scent of stephanotis and realised that
it was twined across an arch where the double ceremony
would have taken place. She breathed in the sensuous
magic of it all, and sighed.

'Make you regret not taking Daniel on?' Andrew murmured in her ear, and she spun around to see the teasing
smile that lurked at the corner of his mouth.

But his eyes were grave, and she sensed that he was
waiting for an answer.

'Not at all,' she said robustly, then she smiled. 'But it
is pretty, isn't it?'

'Very pretty,' he agreed gravely, looking not at the
decorations but at her.

Uneasiness etched its way into the magic of the setting
and she was relieved when Susan swept towards them,
her arms outheld in welcome.

'Oh, Christa! You're just in time to eat. Did your mother
get away safely? Did she enjoy her visit? Come on in and
say hello.'

She paused for a moment and glanced at Andrew, as if
waiting for Christa to introduce her friend, then Christa
saw her blink and look again.

'That was a classic double-take,' she said, smiling at the

older woman. 'You've met Andrew Walsh from Caltura, haven't you, Susan? I found him at the airport and gave him a lift.'

She imagined that she heard a quiet chuckle from Andrew as she repeated the rehearsed words!

'Oh, goodness, yes,' Susan said, holding out a hand to greet Andrew. 'I've met you before, but never looking quite so handsome!'

Totally uninhibited, she examined him from top to toe then nodded her approval.

'Very handsome indeed,' she added, and looked speculatively at Christa.

'Forget it, Susan,' her co-worker said. 'You've had enough weddings for this year, and I've had enough of people trying to arrange my life. That's why I left home, remember?'

'Well, I like that!' Susan said, winking outrageously at Andrew. 'I didn't say a word, now did I?'

Christa moved on towards the party, but she heard him laugh.

'Well, hardly a word,' he agreed, his clear voice reaching out and sensitising her shoulder-blades.

She looked towards the other guests, picking out her colleagues from the Rainbow Bay Base of the Royal Flying Doctor Service, while she tried to escape the faint stirrings Andrew Walsh was causing in her soul.

Jack Gregory, the senior doctor, was talking to Leonie Cooper, the base manager, and they both turned and waved to her as she approached. Eddie Stone, the chief pilot and husband of Susan, was frowning at his handsome twin sons, Lachlan and Stewart, and obviously reading the riot act to them. Beyond them Christa could see Allysha. She was wearing a cream silk suit, and her happiness was almost palpable—even from thirty feet away. Allysha and

Nick—one of the happy couples. Where were Katie and Peter?

'Come and introduce me.'

Andrew must have finished his conversation with Susan for he loomed up beside her and, taking hold of her elbow, he steered her into the centre of the festivities.

'So, how will you manage with two doctors, one pilot and one radio operator all going off honeymooning at the same time?' Andrew asked Leonie, after Christa had performed that introduction.

'It's not as bad as it seems,' Leonie told him. 'Peter had arranged to take two months' leave to attend a trauma response conference in the United States, then go on to Europe to do further aero-medical study. He's due to go in seven weeks and we had already booked a locum to take his place. He and Katie have postponed their honeymoon until then.'

'So, you're only one doctor and one pilot short,' Andrew commented, and Jack nodded and took up the explanations.

'When pilots go on leave Eddie does more flying so we can usually get around that, and we have an ex-RFDS doctor who loves being seconded back to the Service. He doesn't do evacuation or clinic flights any more, but he takes over all the radio and phone consultations. He's here somewhere. Come on, I'll introduce you.'

Christa watched as Jack led Andrew away. She should have been relieved, yet she felt a stirring of. . .emptiness?

Leonie was asking about her mother's visit, and she answered the questions automatically. Maybe it was the dress that was making her feel uncomfortable. Her work uniform of green culottes and a patterned shirt was as 'dressed-up' as she ever wanted to be. Her civilian wardrobe consisted mostly of shorts for summer and jeans for winter, with an assortment of T-shirts that suited both seasons here in the Tropics.

'I'm sorry, Leonie, I wasn't listening.'

She turned back to the base manager, uneasily aware that this distraction was something new.

Leonie smiled at her, then glanced across to where Andrew and Peter were talking to Frank Wiley before she repeated the question.

'I know we shouldn't be talking work, but you were on days off when all this was decided. I wondered if you'd mind staying on at Caltura next week with the eye specialist?'

Christa tried to imagine what had been said before this, but couldn't admit to total inattention.

'Now my mother has gone I could go for six months,' she said jokingly, and was surprised when Leonie reacted with a start.

'Don't say things like that!' she scolded. 'I might have sounded confident about the staff changes when I spoke to Andrew but it's giving me nightmares.' She paused, and glanced across at the three men once again. 'And I've a feeling that's what Andrew wants to talk to Jack about on Monday. I think he wants a nurse out at Caltura, and I wouldn't put it past him to try some poaching.'

Christa felt a jolting disturbance in her chest. She followed Leonie's lead and looked across at the man who had come into Caltura like a spirit wind, stirring the people in the settlement out of a debilitating lethargy and breathing not only new life into the run-down cattle property but a new determination and enthusiasm into the men and women of the out-station.

'There are plenty of nurses willing to work in the outback,' she pointed out.

'At an Aboriginal settlement that has a converted

schoolhouse as a hospital?' Leonie's voice echoed her disbelief.

'It's not nearly as bad as it sounds,' Christa said, defending the work Andrew had done in an incredibly short time. 'It's spotlessly clean, and has a good deal of equipment now.'

Expensive equipment, her inner voice whispered as the questions about Andrew's past pressed to the forefront of her mind again.

'And it's not as isolated as the island communities—only three hours' drive to the nearest town.'

Leonie smiled at her.

'I don't think you've sold it yet,' she remarked. 'Many of the nurses willing to work in the outback are thinking of rich and handsome young men on sheep or cattle properties, not a clean ex-schoolhouse and a town three hours' drive away.'

Christa shrugged, knowing that part of what Leonie said was correct. However, there was something special about Caltura, and she had to defend it.

'But it's a beautiful place,' she argued. 'Admittedly, first impressions are of dust and flies—'

'I've been there,' Leonie put in drily. 'Second, third and fourth impressions are also of dust and flies!'

'That's near the airstrip,' Christa pointed out. 'In fact, that part of the settlement should be moved. About half a mile away, towards the cattle property homestead, the country changes. There's a lagoon with permanent water so you get grass and other vegetation growing, and the birds swoop in at sunset—black against the red night sky. It's a magical place, Leonie, once you get away from the old shacks and shanties of the "village", and take in the subtle beauty of that understated landscape.'

'The lagoon is not a woman's place!'

Andrew's stern statement made her spin around. He'd approached so silently that she'd been unaware of his presence until he spoke.

'I found that out,' she said, and grimaced at him, then turned to Leonie. 'I followed the children there one afternoon and watched them swim, frolicking in the water with such natural grace and athleticism. Then one of the men approached and told me bad things had happened to a young woman there.'

She hesitated for a moment, and looked from Leonie to Andrew before she added, 'He made it OK,' she said, smiling at the man who was fast becoming King of Caltura. 'He rubbed his armpit smell on me to confuse the spirit of the lagoon, so I now have special status with that particular wraith and can wander out there to watch the sunset without upsetting him—or her.'

Leonie made some comment but Christa was watching Andrew, hoping that her story hadn't offended him in any way. He was dark-haired with olive skin that tanned easily, but with his grey eyes and European features it was hard to decide how he fitted into the 'families' at Caltura. He didn't flaunt whatever Aboriginal heritage he might have, but she was certain that he would not have been accepted so readily by the people of the isolated community if he had not been connected by blood somewhere in his ancestry.

'So, you've been accepted to that extent,' he mused after a lengthy silence. He smiled down at her. His features were arranged into a mask of warm approval, but his eyes were so full of appraisal that she found herself suddenly cold in the balmy night air.

Then Katie touched her arm. 'We're sorry you missed the ceremony, but glad you finally made it!'

Christa turned to congratulate the newly-weds, her heart

a little envious of their transparent happiness while her head reminded her that she'd made her choice. Peter began to talk to Andrew, and Katie swept her away to meet her parents.

She mixed and mingled, enjoying the undemanding company of these people with whom she worked. Yet, as she moved through the crowd of friends and acquaintances, she felt separated from the others by a sense of her own 'aloneness'. Even Sally, the young clerical assistant, had a boyfriend with her.

The vaguely dissatisfying thoughts made her smile a little more warmly than usual when Andrew finally reappeared by her side.

'Both bridal couples are leaving,' he informed her. 'Do you want to join in the bouquet-catching mêlée?'

'No thank you,' she said firmly. 'I said goodbye to them all—that's enough.' She caught sight of Sally, pressing through the throng around the two couples. 'Weddings might make some people go all mushy but, considering the divorce statistics these days, they tend to bring out the cynic in me.'

'Perhaps I should catch a bouquet for you,' he suggested, and she looked at him in surprise. 'You're far too young to be cynical.'

'I'm not *that* young,' she muttered, but he wasn't smiling and his eyes had that peculiar, assessing look in them again. 'And I don't want one caught for me. I'm not superstitious, but I'm certainly not going to tempt fate.'

'Would it be such an unendurable fate?' he murmured, his eyes now scanning her face as if he might be able to read an answer on her skin.

The very definite 'yes' that usually sprang to her lips died before it was uttered, and she mumbled something about thanking Susan and hurried away from him.

He was standing by her car when she emerged from the house, after helping her host and hostess with the final cleaning-up. She felt a wave of something she told herself was irritation wash through her body. Andrew Walsh's presence at the celebrations seemed to have affected the atmosphere in some way, infusing a restlessness into it that had transmitted itself into her body.

'My belongings are in the trunk,' he reminded her as she crossed the road towards him.

She looked around. The street that had been lined with cars only hours earlier was now deserted.

Could she let him retrieve his suitcase and drive off, abandoning him out here in the suburbs?

'Where are you staying? I'll give you a lift,' she offered, hoping that he wouldn't divine her reluctance to spend more time alone with him.

'I haven't booked in anywhere, but if you could drop me in town I'll find a hotel. It's only for a few nights. I'm cadging a lift back to Caltura with you people on Tuesday.'

It was like the moment in the air terminal when the world had paused in its spinning for a moment and she'd seen him as the solitary traveller. Only now he was a dark portent, black against the star-filled sky, yet no shadowy power could stop the words already threading their way through the still air towards him.

'You can stay at my place, if you don't mind a puppy that wakes at the unsociable hour of six o'clock,' she said, and saw him nod as if he'd expected the invitation.

'In the spare bedroom,' she added hoarsely—then felt a sudden rush of shame.

As if the man would have expected to stay anywhere else!

CHAPTER TWO

A WILD carillon of bells infiltrated Christa's dream, merging the scene—in the confusing manner of dreams—from a lagoon covered in candles to a flower-decked church. At that stage she woke enough to recognise the noise as real, and reached out for the phone.

'A woman's been brought in to Wooli with heat exhaustion, query heatstroke,' the man on duty at the answering service told her. 'Sister Chapman has her stabilised, but reckons she should come straight to town for tests. I've paged the pilot. Jack's on a flight to the city with a young fellow who came off his motorbike, so you're on your own. You can contact either Jack or Wooli by phone once you're in the air.'

She was out of bed before he finished speaking—crossing to the bathroom, where she rested the mobile phone on the cabinet while she washed her face and brushed her teeth. Being on her own was nothing new. Almost eighty per cent of evacuation flights were carried out with only a nurse on board. It was a matter of continuing whatever treatment the hospital sister had initiated and keeping the patient stable during the flight. She glanced at her watch. Three-thirty! She'd had four hours' sleep, but knew she'd be awake for the day now that she was up and moving.

Back in her bedroom she pulled on a long-sleeved, long-legged cotton tracksuit in a serviceable but smart navy blue. The weather in Rainbow Bay was still hot, but beyond the ranges the nights were getting colder. She tucked the mobile phone in her pocket, pulled a brush through her crop of thick, unruly hair, grabbed her car keys and, remembering her guest, tiptoed softly into the hall.

The light was on in the spare bedroom, and the door opened as she approached.

'Was that a duty call for you?' Andrew asked in a husky murmur, his usually clear tones smudged with sleep.

He was shadowed by the light behind him but, even so, his body—naked, apart from a pair of cartoon-covered boxer shorts—attracted Christa's eyes long enough for an image of muscled strength, satiny skin and an arrowing thatch of sleek dark hair to be imprinted in her mind.

'I'm on call, so it was to be expected,' she explained. 'I'm sorry it disturbed you.'

'Don't be sorry—take me with you. Two seconds to grab some clothes and I'll dress in the car.'

Still mesmerised by the bare chest, she nodded and then, as he disappeared back into the spare bedroom, she realised that she must be mad.

'This against regulations?' he asked, guessing her thoughts as she hurried out to the car.

'Not entirely. We sometimes take journalists or photographers, and often include visiting medical staff. I suppose, as health worker at Caltura, you could qualify.'

But his presence disturbed her more than the phone call, moving about in the car as he shrugged his body into clothes. She concentrated on the road to chase away the re-awakening fantasies.

He didn't speak, yet she could feel his presence beating against her skin.

Something had been buzzing in the air around her since she'd met him at the airport yesterday. Pheromones, her more enlightened friends would tell her, clinically defined as compounds given out by animals in response to a stimulant—such as sex! She'd never believed a word of it!

Until now. . .

'All dressed and respectable,' he announced as she drew up in the parking area.

Bill had the plane out of the hangar, and she parked beside the fence and hurried inside to get the equipment and drugs she would need.

'Come on—hangers-on are expected to make themselves useful.'

Emergency supplies were kept in special packs, their contents replaced and double-checked after each flight. She selected the drugs she thought she might find useful, added some ice packs from the freezer and relocked the cabinets.

Andrew lifted both bags and she followed him out, thankful that all the planes were now fitted not only with oxygen and suction but with a portable vital signs monitor and a defibrillator so she didn't have to carry those as well.

'Joyrider?' Bill teased, and Christa was thankful for the darkness that hid the wash of heat in her cheeks. The two men greeted each other, then Andrew led the way into the plane. He dropped the equipment case on the stretcher, and looked around the specially fitted interior.

'It never ceases to amaze me—the way you can convert the small space in these cabins to so many uses.'

Bill, following Christa up the steps, nodded. 'I guess we all take it for granted.' He closed the door and locked it. 'We'll be an hour,' he told his passengers, 'if you want to get some sleep on the way. This isn't exactly what the doctor ordered after a big night out, is it?'

He grinned sympathetically at them, and walked through to the cockpit. Christa secured the equipment with Velcro straps, thought about the possibilities of sleep and decided that it would be pointless. Once again she was trapped in a small space with a man whose body was bombarding hers with silent messages.

'Why don't you go up front with Bill?' she suggested, but Andrew shook his head.

'I'll take the offer of an hour's sleep, thanks. It's been a rare commodity these last few days.' He strapped himself into one of the seats and closed his eyes.

Why had he come? she wondered. And why were there always more questions than answers where Andrew was concerned?

Feeling slightly rejected, she went up to take the copilot's seat. Flying at night had a magic all of its own, a magic that two years with the RFDS had done nothing to diminish.

They dropped down to the strip at Wooli in the deeper darkness that seemed to precede the dawn, and while Bill and Andrew helped the 'ambulance' driver transfer the patient from the battered old vehicle to the plane Christa spoke to Val Chapman.

'The patient is one of a group of southerners who come up regularly to fish the gulf rivers,' Val explained. 'They camp near the Brealla River for about a month. Apparently, our patient went out with her husband yesterday but the fish weren't biting and she became bored. He put her ashore and she decided to walk back to the camp, but lost her way. According to his calculations, it was only a couple of miles but she was walking for at least four hours.'

'I can't believe this,' Christa muttered. 'No matter how well they think they know the area, people shouldn't be walking about out here on their own. How hot was it yesterday?'

Val echoed her sigh.

'We've had close to forty-degree Celsius temperatures every day, but, because the nights are cold and the early mornings are cool visitors don't seem to realise how hot it gets in the afternoon. She did have enough sense to head back to the tree-band by the river when she realised she was lost, and eventually made it back to the camp-site. She felt sick and had a headache so she lay down.'

'Was she conscious when she arrived at the hospital? Did she tell you all of this?'

Val shook her head. 'Her husband heard the story from two other women who had stayed at the camp. They spoke to her when she returned and offered her food and drinks.'

'And?' Christa prompted as Bill signalled that he was ready to go.

'When her husband returned at night fall she had become disorientated, and was talking what he called "nonsense". He put her in the car, and by the time they reached me—it's a two-hour drive—she was unresponsive. The file will fill you in on what's happened since then. Good luck!'

Christa moved towards the plane then stopped and looked around, realising that they had only the one passenger. She called to Val, who was heading for the ambulance.

'Where's her husband now?' she asked, surprised that the man hadn't accompanied his wife. Maybe he would drive back to the coast—although it would be a long trip on his own.

'Oh, he's gone back to the camp,' Val replied. 'Once he'd delivered her to hospital he felt he'd done his bit. I reckon he was gone before I'd intubated her. He probably decided that if the barramundi weren't biting yesterday he'd be sure to catch some this morning!'

Christa shook her head as she climbed into the plane.

'No wonder I'm a cynic about marriage,' she muttered to Bill and Andrew. 'Let's go!'

She looked down at the large woman who lay so limply

on the stretcher, unaware that her husband had abandoned her to return to his sport.

'I'll look after you,' she promised the stranger, although she realised that the woman would be unaware of her voice or presence.

'You really care about her in a personal way, don't you?' Andrew asked, and she was shocked by the surprise in his voice.

'Of course I care! Isn't there enough misery and unhappiness in the world without people deliberately inflicting more on each other through thoughtless or selfish acts?'

She checked the IV tubes and bag, attached the leads to monitor her patient's heartbeat and oxygenation, directed the aircraft's air vents so that they blew directly onto the damp sheet that covered her body and then unhooked the file clipped to the side of the stretcher.

Andrew strapped himself into a seat and watched her, but the rhythm of her work was acting as a buffer between them. As long as she concentrated on that she could ignore the capricious responses of her body.

She read through the file while Bill took off, knowing that she would have to do a full assessment of her patient once they were in the air.

Candy Delpratt. Christa checked her patient again, wondering if the name had suited a younger version of the greying, overweight woman on the stretcher.

She'd been admitted with a rectal temperature of 41°C which had come down to 39.5°C on Val's last reading thirty minutes ago. Flushed skin, tongue dry and leathery, no oedema, no external trauma. Christa filed the information away in her mind, knowing that it would help her make decisions later. Breath sounds clear, heart sounds normal, no known allergies—according to the absent husband.

'We're up,' Bill called back to her and she unclipped her seatbelt and moved across to her patient, speaking to her first in the hope that she might respond.

'Can I help?' Andrew asked, and Christa considered.

'I need to cool her—that and replacing fluid are the two most important things at this stage. You could open the larger of the two equipment bags. It has the cold pack in it. I'll want five ice packs.'

He moved away, and Christa began her assessment.

The sheet had dried and grown warm so she removed it, knowing that it would prevent any further evaporation. Val had packed a second damp sheet, and she drew it up over her patient.

Explaining what she was doing, she suctioned out the airway, moistened the woman's body with a damp cloth and replaced the ice packs at her patient's neck, armpits and groin areas.

'Will she be OK?' Andrew asked, standing to one side so that Christa could move freely.

'Her temperature's dropping, which is a good sign, but it's not low enough to stop cooling measures yet.'

The phone rang in her pocket, and she fished it out and flipped it open.

'How's your patient?' Jack asked and Christa smiled, pleased to find that he was monitoring her even while involved in his own emergency.

'Val fitted a Foley catheter, but Mrs Delpratt's urine output is very low, and the colour's a dark greenish-brown. She's on 5% dextrose in .45% saline IV. Should I give her mannitol to maintain adequate urine flow?'

'I think so.' Jack's voice was crisp and clear. 'Do you have her approximate weight? The measure for mannitol is 1mg per kilogram administered over a twenty-four hour period, but try a test dose first. You're aiming for a urine flow of 30 to 50ml an hour. Start with a 75ml dose in a 20% solution and administer it slowly—over three to five minutes. If the urine flow doesn't improve try another test dose, then leave it for the hospital after that.'

Christa jotted the measurements on the file. It was a practice she'd carried out many times, but she felt more secure under Jack's supervision.

'What about electrolyte and acid imbalances?' she asked.

'There's not much anyone can do about that, apart from fluid replacement, until she gets to hospital and they do lab tests on her blood and know what's happening. As well as renal failure, there's always a chance of liver damage. Keep an eye on her ECG for any signs of dysrhythmia. Is she responding to external cooling?'

'Yes,' Christa assured him, knowing that physical lowering of the patient's temperature would relieve the need for drugs which could cause other complications in her already distressed body.

'You're doing fine, then,' he said. 'Phone me if there are any other problems.'

She said goodbye and checked her patient.

Andrew was wiping the woman's face with a damp cloth and, for a moment, Christa was struck by the gentle movement of his strong, work-roughened hands.

Mannitol! she reminded herself. She glanced at the file. Val had written Candy's weight down as eighty kilograms—a figure she'd have been given by Mr Delpratt or had estimated herself. Looking at the patient, she decided that it was close to correct and drew up the test dose, noted the time and urine volume then fed the medication slowly into the drip.

Any increase in urine output would be imperceptible at first so, while Andrew once again stood aside, she began another assessment—checking pulse and blood pressure, temperature and respiration and noting down all the findings on the patient file.

'You enjoy it, don't you?'

The question made her turn towards their passenger.

'I suppose I do,' she admitted, although she rarely analysed her own reactions to her job. 'I like the one-to-one contact with the patient. In this case, joining in her battle back towards stability and assisting it in a positive way.'

'But there's no follow-up work. Once your patient is loaded into an ambulance, you've lost her.'

'True, in some ways,' she granted him. 'Although we do phone the hospital and check, and often receive a thank-you note that tells us what happened later, but there's a different pleasure in the battle against the combined odds of illness or trauma and the complication of distance.'

'Different enough to make RFDS nursing your life's work?'

'ETA ten minutes. I've alerted the ambulance.' Bill's voice saved her from replying immediately, but the question was perplexing.

'I don't know about "life's work"! Who thinks quite that far ahead?'

She looked up from the notes she'd been writing, and peered towards the cockpit. Dawn was breaking over the bay, painting the undersides of the clouds with soft pink, and rose and gold—gentle, rainbow colours welcoming another day. She'd heard that there was a story about a Rainbow Spirit—a native legend that had led to the naming of the town she now called home.

Would Andrew know it? she wondered. She turned to ask him, then felt a curious throb of excitement as an image of his naked chest replaced the glory of the sunrise in her mind's eye. She blinked, saw the decently dressed comparative stranger in the seat behind her and turned quickly away again.

Enough of that, she told herself as the plane touched down. There's work to be done.

Candy Delpratt's temperature remained above normal so Christa replaced the warming ice packs once again, then tucked a clean sheet around the woman for her journey to hospital. She checked the fluid lines and fixed the bag to the stand attached to the stretcher, noted her patient's vital signs once more and detached the monitor. Urine output had increased with the test dose of mannitol, and she wrote a note to that effect on the file.

Finally she placed the bag containing the patient's personal toiletries and clothing under the sheet at the end of the stretcher, and Candy was set for transfer.

The plane drew up outside their hangar, and she saw the ambulance bearers move towards it. She opened the door to let them in.

'All ready to go?' the young attendant asked as he bounded up the steps.

'All ready,' Christa responded, removing her copy of the patient file and handing the rest to the newcomer. 'Heatstroke—all the details and the transfer forms from Wooli are there.'

Bill was releasing the stretcher from its anchoring points when the second attendant arrived. Christa watched as they slid the stretcher off the rails and manoeuvred it out of the door. Some of the newer planes in other states were fitted with hoists, which made this part of the job easier. Once the stretcher was out of the plane the legs and wheels dropped down to take the weight of the patient, but nothing had been invented—yet—to wheel them down the steps at the angle they needed to work through the door!

'See you again soon,' the younger attendant called, and Christa waved.

'Not today, I hope,' Bill muttered. 'I was looking forward to a slothful Sunday.' He turned his head and scanned the clear morning sky, its pale blue beauty enhanced by the white fluff of clouds along the horizon. 'It's going to be a great one. Have you two got plans?'

The question jolted Christa, and she was very pleased that Andrew had followed the ambulance men out of the plane—out of earshot.

'I don't know what Andrew's doing,' she said quickly, hoping to break any link Bill might have imagined between them. She tidied up the cabin. 'I might drive up the coast.'

She spoke the thought aloud, and felt her body respond with a pulse-quickening thrill of anticipation as she imagined herself asking Andrew to accompany her; predicted his pleased acceptance and her own pleasure in taking him to the deserted beaches and hidden groves of rain-forest which had become her favourite haunts.

Perhaps she'd been celibate for too long, her saner self suggested, for images of a bare-chested male—in conjunction with deserted beaches—had set her heart fluttering!

She finished her work and left the plane, convinced that the silly mood was her mother's fault. All the talk of old friends' new babies and Daniel's exploits had unsettled her.

'I'd better come back with you and get my gear,' Andrew said, and she wondered if he was in a hurry to leave her place. Or had she only invited him to stay the one night? She couldn't remember.

She looked into his grey eyes, but they were unreadable.

Forget deserted beaches, her mind warned.

'And have some breakfast,' she suggested, knowing that

she was pleased to have his company, in spite of the
warning voice. 'Helpers deserve breakfast.'

He took her keys to unlock the car while she refilled
drug packs and locked the cabinets. As he opened the
driver's side door for her she felt special. It was nice to
be fussed over, she decided.

But don't get used to it! the inner voice warned. The
man has good manners, that's all!

Turning into her street, she experienced her usual rush of
affection for the old worker's cottage that was her snug
home. It was a symbol of her independence and, today, it
represented security.

'It's a neat little place now I see it in daylight,' Andrew
remarked, giving her an absurd sense of pleasure.

She smiled as she stopped outside, knowing that she
would probably need the car later.

An excited barking greeted her and Wally came tearing
around the house, long ears flapping around his face and
his mouth open so that he looked as if he was smiling.

'The dog that wakes at dawn?'

'The very same!' she agreed, and tried to stop the puppy
leaping all over their unexpected guest.

'Wally!' she said sternly. The little dog immediately
sank to the ground and slid towards her in an attitude of
cowed repentance.

She watched the performance for a moment, then said,
'Get up, you ridiculous animal. You don't fool me for one
moment.'

As Wally leapt to his feet and cavorted around her she
heard her houseguest laugh—a warm, rich sound that filled
the morning with joy. The dog, sensing a friend, dashed
off—returning to lay a tattered, wet-looking ball at
Andrew's feet.

Christa looked up and caught the smile that lingered on Andrew's face. And, at that moment, she finally admitted that the heart-fluttering excitement she was experiencing had nothing to do with her mother's visit!

She watched the play of muscles in his chest, emphasised by the thin knitted shirt, as he twisted his torso and flung the ball towards the far fence for Wally to chase.

'Good throw?' he asked, turning towards her with a wide grin.

'Not bad at all,' she repeated, thinking of his physique — not his pitching prowess — while her head cautioned her to remember the 'prolonged celibacy' explanation for this uncharted interest.

'I guess I'd better get cleaned up,' she added hurriedly—anything to get away from him for a while and straighten things out in her mind.

'Well, if you don't mind my invading your kitchen, I'll rustle up some breakfast for us while you shower. Off you go.'

Astonishment widened her eyes, and he grinned.

'I'm quite handy around the place, you know!' He turned away, and retrieved the ball Wally had dropped at his feet.

'Good dog! That's enough,' he told the pup. 'You have a rest and I might take you for a walk later.'

To Christa's surprise, Wally dropped immediately to the ground. She stared at her excitable animal, unable to believe his docile obedience to a stranger.

And was she supposed to fall into line as meekly? Off you go, indeed! She pushed a hand through her hair, easing the tangle of curls off her forehead. Did she look a mess that he was suggesting a shower? Not that she didn't want to bathe and change into something clean, and cooler.

She glanced at him, but the grey eyes were as clear as

spring water—guileless, almost! His lips lifted at one side, tilting into a half-smile—challenging her to argue.

'I'm on my way!' she assured him, refusing the dare. 'No doubt you'll find the kitchen!'

She hurried past him into the house, furious with herself for such docility. It was her place, after all! What right did Andrew Walsh have to be ordering her around in it? And ordering her dog around as well!

The smell of bacon crisping overcame her irritation, and she emerged from the shower and hurriedly pulled on her most comfortable white cut-off denim shorts and a blue and white striped T-shirt. She smoothed moisturiser onto her face, rubbing it in around the corners of her eyes where tiny lines might be expected to appear.

Her hair clung damply to her forehead and temples and she pushed it back with a navy-blue band, revealing her wide brow and deep-set dark eyes.

'You're not bad-looking for someone whose mother considers that she's on the shelf,' she told her reflection, taking in the neat nose and full, nicely shaped lips. Her skin was her best asset, she decided, continuing the dispassionate appraisal. Smooth and clear, it tanned easily— giving her a healthy, wholesome look.

Wholesome? she wondered. Was that what men were looking for? And why, after all this time, was she suddenly concerned with what men were looking for in a woman?

'Breakfast's ready!'

Her heart's response supplied the answer.

Surely it was just the proximity of this man in her house—the fact that the pheromones couldn't escape as they did outdoors! Maybe the dust diminished their effect at Caltura, she decided, and grinned to herself.

'It smells delicious,' she said, entering her own kitchen as a stranger and sitting at the place he indicated at her own table.

He sniffed the air.

'And so do you,' he murmured, a teasing gleam clearly visible in his dark-lashed eyes.

'Are you flirting with me?' she asked, her heartbeat accelerating wildly.

He placed a plate of bacon, scrambled eggs and grilled tomatoes in front of her, then looked down at her upturned face and smiled.

'Thank goodness you recognised it,' he said, his lips twitching with merriment. 'It's been so long, I thought I might have forgotten how.'

His reply stunned her into silence—for a moment, at least! Then, as she began to eat, some sanity returned.

He sat opposite her, and attacked his breakfast with enthusiasm. His attention to the food gave her the opportunity to study him more closely. In the months she had known him he had always been polite, enthusiastic about rebuilding Caltura, a willing worker and eager to learn all he could about medical matters. She had walked with him after dinner some nights, listening to him talk about his plans, but he had always been. . . She searched for the word.

Remote—that was it. A little detached, as if he was willing to be part of the business side of their contact but wished to remain aloof from social obligations of any kind—not even giving enough of himself for their relationship to grow beyond the most platonic of friendships.

'Why?' she asked, as her scrutiny and accompanying thoughts provided no obvious solution to this totally unexpected attitudinal change.

He looked up and chuckled, but she read the expression in his eyes as wary, not amused.

'Blunt, and to the point, eh?' he teased, then studied her in turn before he spoke again.

'I feel attracted to you,' he eventually declared, in much the same way, Christa thought, as someone might say, 'I'm fond of apples'.

She busied herself buttering toast while searching for a response more appropriate than the disbelieving, 'Oh, really!' which had sprung to her lips.

'It's a bit sudden, isn't it?' she finally managed, then the absurdity of the situation struck her and she choked on a gurgle of laughter, winning an answering smile from Andrew—and this time it did reach his eyes, enveloping her in the subtle warmth of complicity.

'Sudden but possible, wouldn't you say?' he replied, and a husky undertone in his voice etched its way along Christa's nerves. She knew, without a doubt, that he was deliberately seducing her, projecting his appeal to entangle all her senses in his potent sexuality.

And her body was falling for it! Warming to his voice; quickening beneath the blatant challenge in his eyes; eating up the waves of awareness as greedily as she'd attacked the breakfast he'd prepared.

She tried to ignore the traitorous excitement and looked at the cause of it again, determined to be sensible—to analyse what was happening here before she lost all control! Could a man turn such a powerful force on and off at will?

He had lifted a piece of toast to his lips and she watched as he bit into it, strong white teeth visible for an instant. Then his beautifully contoured lips covered them, and his mouth moved with a mesmerising grace. Her body rejected her silent cautions, warming to a tingling excitement at the

unexpected sensuality a shared breakfast could evoke—
imagining that mouth moving on hers. . .

'You're not exactly fending me off,' he remarked when
the toast had been despatched. She saw his eyes move and
knew that he was studying her as closely as she had studied
him. Were her cheeks flushed? Her eyes glistening with
desire? Could he see her arousal as clearly as she could
see—and feel—his concentrated onslaught on her senses?

'I don't know that I could,' she murmured, while his
steady scrutiny intensified her reactions and she wanted to
run her hands over her body to ease a forceful, aching need.

'We're both adults. Unattached?' He made the final
word a question and she nodded, although she knew that
her assent would only take her deeper into this unfamiliar
territory. 'Would it be so wrong?'

As he said the words he rose, and moved around the
table towards her. For a moment she thought that he might
bend to kiss her, for his gaze held hers and she had to
turn her head to follow his approach. He reached her side,
and placed a hand on her shoulder. She felt a powerful
jolt along her nerves, as if the touch had completed
an electrical circuit and the current had hit her with
unnerving force.

It's his closeness—having a man in the house—that's
unsettling, she told herself, but suspected that wasn't
entirely true.

'Let's go for a drive,' she croaked when her breathing
had stabilised enough for her to form the words. Another
few minutes in the house and they'd be in bed together!
And she needed time to think before she took that
particular leap.

'Coward!' he murmured, but his hand left her shoulder
and he leaned over and picked up her plate, reaching across

the table to stack his own on top and carrying both to the sink.

Christa watched him move away. He was casually dressed but the clothes he'd chosen to wear did nothing to diminish the attractiveness of his broad shoulders and tapering waist—while the well-cut shorts only emphasised the attraction of his—

Heavens! She'd end up in bed with him tonight for sure, the way her thoughts were running. But she was twenty-seven, not a twitty teenager turned on by a man's tempting body, and for years she'd avoided entanglements that led to bed.

He turned, and caught her absent-minded appraisal.

'Where shall we drive?' he asked, lifting a teatowel and drying the dishes while he waited for her reply.

'I thought up the coast a little way,' she said, giving up the idea of deserted beaches and deciding instead on a newly developed and very trendy meeting-place. 'Have you been to The Cove?'

He shook his head, a suspicious little smile playing about his lips.

'I'm a southerner,' he reminded her. 'I don't know the area at all, but I assume "The Cove" is well populated?'

She felt embarrassment heat her cheeks and lifted her hands to press her fingers against them, while her lips responded to his smile.

'Very well populated,' she acknowledged, then admitted, 'I need time to think, Andrew.'

'You've got all day,' he promised, and he put down the plate he was drying and stepped towards her.

She stiffened, preparing her body for another onslaught when he touched her, but he paused at arm's length and added, 'That's if you're still willing to offer me hospitality.'

'I'll think about that too,' she told him, but she knew that he'd detected the uncertainty in her voice. Her body didn't need to think about anything, but her mind was warning her to wait—at least until she'd had time apart from him to think things through without the weakening tumult of her senses which his presence had activated.

And time to find an answer to a few other overwhelming questions—like, why was he doing this? Why her? Why now?

CHAPTER THREE

LITTLE things about Andrew pleased her, Christa decided as she sat back in the passenger seat and let him drive the short distance north. Offering to drive, for instance, and suggesting that they take Wally—who now lay, panting with canine delight, on a towel in the back seat.

'Should you be sleeping?' he asked, glancing across at her.

She shook her head.

'Once I'm up, I'm up,' she told him. 'I might rest this afternoon if I don't have another call.'

She felt his reaction in the slowing of the car.

'You're on call today as well?' he demanded, as if such a thing were inconceivable.

'Twenty-four hour shift,' she told him, smiling at his patent astonishment. 'I started at six last night and could have had to whisk away at any stage during the wedding celebrations.'

'Then how come we're heading off for an outing?'

She smiled again, and patted the small leather pouch she had dropped at her feet.

'I've got the mobile phone in my bag. The Cove is within a half-hour's drive of the airport, and that's my limit of movement. It takes that long for the pilot to get there, and do his pre-flight checks. All we medical staff have to do is arrive, grab whatever drugs or equipment we might need and hop on board.'

Watching his face, as she explained, she imagined she saw it stiffen, but when he turned to her again his eyes

were twinkling. He nodded towards the little bag and murmured, 'So, you could still be saved by the bell.'

'More than likely,' she agreed. 'We do have slow days,
but the Base averages four evacuations a day throughout
the year so we have to be busy some of the time.'

He didn't reply, and they drove in silence until they
reached The Cove turn-off. It was as if he was assimilating
the information—or was he restructuring some plans? A
cool slide of apprehension mingled with the hot desire his
body continued to kindle within her without any apparent
effort on his part.

He swung the car towards the beach, found a parking
space at one end of the paved street then turned towards
her, once again dominating all the space in the small car.

'There'll be other days,' he said softly, his eyes fixed
on hers, reiterating the promise.

Wally broke the spell, leaping into the space between
them and demanding his freedom. Christa clipped on his
lead, jammed a wide-brimmed raffia hat on her head, slung
her bag over her shoulder and opened the door to let him
out. She felt as if she were escaping from something,
although, if asked, she would not have been able to explain
the feeling.

'Very domestic, this walking the dog on the beach.'
Andrew put her thoughts into words, but they were
thoughts she didn't want to acknowledge. 'And it's an
interesting place.'

He was looking away from the water towards the fringe
of pandanus palms and huge old ti trees that hid the mixture of old beach houses and new, low-rise development.
Beneath the trees people strolled or sat at tables beneath
wide canvas umbrellas and sipped coffee.

'Come on, let's have a closer look,' he suggested when

they reached the high timber jetty that pushed out into the sea.

She followed him up the beach, and took the hand he held out to help her clamber onto the low rock wall at the landward end of the jetty. Warmth crept into her skin— warmth and something else that activated tiny pulses in her nerve endings.

Hand in hand, they joined the strollers. Christa looked out towards the blue-green water, seeing the cove and its sheltering islands framed by the trees and marvelling at the beauty of the creamy pink strips of paper-like bark that hung from the ti tree trunks.

'There's a wealth of opportunity here for more planned development.'

Andrew's words brought her out of her nature-induced reverie and she looked around at the buildings, startled that he could be thinking of 'development' while she was absorbing the natural splendour of the place. It reminded her that she knew so little about the person whose hand was sending such startling messages through her system.

'You're interested in development?' she asked, trying to readjust her image of him yet again. In less than twenty-four hours she'd had to accept that the knockabout worker she knew from Caltura had another persona who flew up from Melbourne with expensive designer clothes packed in his leather luggage. And that the 'colleague' with whom she had worked, on and off for two months, was suddenly exerting a devastating effect on her hormones!

'I've done a bit from time to time,' he answered in an offhand manner. 'Good money in it if you choose the right time and the right place.'

The man who chased wild cattle through the scrub on his dirt-bike and worked physically hard from dawn to dusk to pull a run-down property out of the red had access to the kind of money 'development' required?

She was trying to assimilate this new knowledge—to fit it into her slim store of information about him—when Wally took exception to a remark that a spaniel made in passing, and by the time the altercation had been resolved her next question had been forgotten.

Andrew had released her hand to separate the dogs, and now waved towards a vacant table set outside a smart café.

'Shall we have coffee?' he suggested, and Christa, beset by an undefined uneasiness, agreed.

She ordered cappuccino, but as the foaming cup of fragrant coffee was placed in front of her the phone rang.

'It's Jack, Christa. How soon can you get to the airport?'

'I'm at The Cove,' she told him. 'Twenty minutes?'

'Good girl,' he said crisply. 'I'll explain when I see you.'

'I've got to go.' She turned apologetically towards Andrew.

He was already on his feet, digging into his fob pocket for change to pay for their untouched coffees.

'I can get a cab. That way, you could take a look around the village and drive home later,' she suggested, but he shook his head.

'I'll drop you off, then Wally and I will go back to your place and console each other.'

His smile, both mischievous and promising, triggered all the strange responses that his touch had started earlier, and she hurried away lest he read her reaction in her eyes or touched her again and felt it tingling on her skin.

'Why Wally?' he asked as they drove towards the airport and, relieved to have a non-personal conversation, she told him about her acquisition of the dog when a small boy had brought Wally's mother to one of their clinics, suffering from mastitis.

'The island is called Coorawalla, so I thought Wally

would be appropriate!' she explained, hoping that her voice did not betray her agitation. The usual rush of adrenalin an evac flight prompted was mixing with the silent messages from Andrew's body, sharpening all her senses until she seemed already joined to him in some way.

Relief flowed through her when she saw the airport, and she directed him along the perimeter road that led to the RFDS hangar.

'Will you phone when you get back?' he asked as he braked to a halt outside the building. 'I'll come and get you.'

Christa studied him for a moment, striving to accept—and understand—the giant leap their relationship had taken in less than twenty-four hours.

'Someone will drop me home,' she told him. 'I'm sorry I've interrupted your day. Please take the car if you want to go anywhere else. Drop Wally back at the house, and have a good look around the Bay on your own.'

He seemed to consider her suggestion, looking out through the windscreen of the car, his straight profile unreadable. Then he turned and smiled—a brilliant, five-hundred-watt effort that made her blink with its sudden radiance.

'I'll find something to do with myself,' he promised. He reached out and touched her arm.

'Good luck,' he said again and—after she'd opened the door and climbed out—he started the engine, reversed out of the parking bay and drove away.

Jack emerged from the hangar, carrying the bulky Thomas pack, and Christa's heart sank. The pack contained all the equipment needed to save a life, but taking it usually mean that they were heading for a road accident.

'What else do you want?' she asked him, walking towards the hangar.

'Just see if there's anything edible in the fridge—it could be a long afternoon. I've put the drug case on board already and Michael's done his checks, so we can get going.'

She found sandwiches in the freezer and pulled out six packs. Who knew how many passengers they might be bringing back? Or how far they were going? Had Bill been called out on another flight, or would this trip have taken him over his regulation flying hours for the day? There would be a reason why Michael was piloting them when Bill was first on call.

She found a bottle of orange juice in the refrigerator and she put that, with the sandwiches, into a small flight bag.

Jack had the equipment secured by the time she reached the cabin and he closed the door and waved her to a seat, calling to Michael that they were ready to go.

'OK,' Christa said as the plane began to move, 'tell me the worst.'

Jack grinned at her. 'You're always so calm,' he said, and she didn't contradict him, although this morning's experience had proved otherwise. 'And, perhaps, it's just as well because I don't like the sound of this one at all.'

'Road accident?' Christa queried, and was surprised when he shook his head.

'No,' he said grimly. 'It's an accident at a bore-sinking camp. Have you been out to one of them before?'

'I've heard of them,' she replied, 'and know the drillers are usually solitary people who work around the outback, divining for water and then sinking the bores.'

'These days most of them also erect the windmills that drive the pumps to bring the water to the surface, and they put in concrete tanks for the cattle as well. Our patient is one of the best of them, a chap called Warren Fielding. He has modern equipment, a comfortable caravan and a powerful four-wheel-drive vehicle. He's organised enough to camp out in isolated areas for months. He searches for the place where the artesian water is closest to the surface so he can sink the most cost-effective bore.'

Christa waited. Jack always told a story in his own way, and she knew that his lead-up would give her special knowledge of the patient they were about to see.

'His wife and young lad travel with him and, whenever possible, they set up camp within driving distance of a town and close to an old airstrip or near flat ground.'

'Where we can reach him in an emergency,' Christa remarked. 'That's sensible thinking.'

'Oh, he's a modern bushman,' Jack agreed, 'but accidents still happen.'

He went on to explain how Warren and his son had gone out to service a bore he'd put in some years earlier, riding their off-road bikes across the salt-bush plains, while Mrs Fielding drove into the nearest town to replenish the food supplies.

'Warren climbed up to the platform to grease the metal core of the sails, and somehow slipped and fell.'

Christa's stomach clenched. She'd seen the mills, dotted like solitary sentinels across the wide, brown land they called 'the outback'. They were the height of a three- or four-storey building, and interlaced with steel supporting struts. Depending on what he'd hit as he fell, the injuries could be merely bad, or very bad, or horrific.

'How old is the boy?' she asked, and saw a shadow cross Jack's face.

'He's ten, and as plucky a kid as you could get,' he said. 'I spoke to him on the radio when the emergency call came through. His voice was trembling with shock, but he'd had the presence of mind to cover his father with an old towel they carry as a rag, fix some shade over his face, wet his shirt and put it on his dad's lips and leave a water-bottle within reach.

'Then he hopped on his bike and headed back to camp. He hit the alarm button and kept repeating their call sign until I arrived at the Base.'

'Will he wait at the camp to guide us back to his father? And when's his mother due home? Can he contact her?'

Jack held up his hand, as if to say, 'one question at a time', but Christa's heart was full of apprehension—not for the injured man, but for the child who was waiting for help to arrive.

'I've contacted the policeman at Carlisle, where Mrs Fielding goes to shop. He'll track her down and probably drive back to the camp with her. I told the lad—Adam, his name is—that we would be there by two o'clock. He said he wouldn't have time to go out to his father and get back in that time, so he's waiting at the camp.

'The strip is marked because Warren has had equipment flown in to it recently, and he had the map co-ordinates printed above the radio should they ever be needed in an emergency. Adam read them out to me.'

'Sensible father—but what a great kid,' Christa murmured, amazed at the maturity the boy had shown in handling the emergency.

'I'll say,' Jack agreed. 'Now all he's got to do is hold it together until we arrive. He's the only one who can guide us to the patient. Can you ride a dirt-bike?'

Christa nodded. 'They were the only transport available for the nursing staff when I first went to Caltura. If I had to visit someone at the out-station it was ride the bike or walk the couple of miles.'

For a moment she pictured herself riding across the trackless plains and excitement stirred within her, then reality kicked in. 'How far is the camp from Carlisle? If

Mrs Fielding's not back with a vehicle how are we going to transport a patient with probable spine and pelvic injuries on a motorbike?'

'I've been thinking about that,' Jack responded gloomily. 'But we'll have two bikes, so I suppose we'll manage. The town is close to three hours' drive away. Supposing the policeman found her immediately and they set out, we'd still be waiting at least an hour before a vehicle arrived—and we might not have that much time.'

Christa drew in a deep breath, glad that it was Jack with her on this trip. He was the unflappable one, and seven years' experience with the service had taught him the benefits of lateral thinking in awkward situations.

She left him mulling over the problem, and rested her head against the head-rest, thinking she might doze until they landed. But closing her eyes brought Andrew's face into sharp focus, as if it had been flashed up on her eyelids like a transparency on a screen. She remembered the moment in the kitchen when she had thought that he would kiss her, and felt again the momentary regret and then the sizzling excitement of his touch—an electric charge more potent than any kiss.

She was still puzzling over the the shifting balances between them when she felt the wheels bounce on the uneven ground. She switched her thoughts back to work, and wondered about the young boy she was about to meet. Shock could have set in while he waited for the plane—two hours was a long time for a small boy to sit around, worrying.

Jack set out the light stretcher and shouldered the Thomas pack, while Michael taxied towards the caravan with its subsidiary tents and wide canvas awning. As Christa swung the drug case onto her shoulder a small figure emerged, waving what looked like a dishcloth.

Peering through the window, she could see two dust-
embellished motorbikes pulled up in the shade of the van.
Had the father miraculously recovered and ridden back to
camp, or did Mrs Fielding also have a bike?

'I've filled the bikes with petrol and made sandwiches
if you want something to eat,' the youngster said as they
walked down the steps, squinting against the bright
sunshine.

Christa felt her heart squeeze painfully as she pictured
the child, filling in the time by preparing food for them.

'We'll have the sandwiches after we've seen your dad,'
Jack assured him, reaching out to rest one hand casually
on the boy's shoulder. Christa knew that it was a diagnostic
touch, as well as comfort. Jack would feel for tremors in
the boy's slender frame, and check if shock had left him
cold and clammy.

He walked across to the bikes, seemingly satisfied, and
turned to the boy—treating him as he would an adult.

'Now, I've got the pack on my back so how about you
drive and I sit behind you? Have you left a note for your
mother, telling her where we are going?'

Adam nodded.

'Well, in that case, let's go. Michael, you and Christa
will have to share the second bike.'

Christa turned to Michael, who was holding the light-
framed stretcher. 'I'd better drive,' she suggested and
smiled when he groaned and shuddered, muttering smart
remarks about women drivers.

They set off. Christa was tentative at first, feeling her
way across the hard-baked earth and content to keep the
dust-cloud of the first bike in sight.

'Brave kid!' Michael shouted in her ear as they jolted
over old cattle tracks, and the remote emptiness of the
region made the boy's effort all the more remarkable.

It was thirty minutes before they saw the skeletal shape of the windmill, and another ten before they drew up beside the third bike in a scrap of shade provided by the pump housing.

'Fluid, Christa!' Jack's order was crisp and sharp, but relief shot through her as she found the bag and tore open the infusion pack to fit the tubes and catheter to it. You didn't give fluid to dead men!

Warren Fielding was conscious, his face grey with pain, but trying to smile—to talk—as he clung to the hand of his son. Christa saw tears fill the boy's eyes then overflow, marking little tracks down his dust-caked cheeks.

While Jack fitted the drip she reached out and drew Adam close.

'He's going to be OK,' she told him. 'You got help to him in time.'

Jack was talking to the man and the boy turned and buried his tear-stained face in Christa's shirt, sobbing out all his fear and tension now that someone else had taken over.

'OK, Adam,' Jack said briskly. 'How about you lend a hand here?'

The boy wiped his sleeve across his eyes and sniffed, then straightened up and turned to Jack—a man again, ready to take on his responsibilities.

'Hold the bag,' Jack told him, and he stood beside his father's prone figure and held the bag aloft while Jack probed at Warren's body, questioning the man in a quiet, unconcerned voice.

'Now, I'll immobilise Warren's head while you fit a collar, Christa,' Jack said, 'then we'll slide the stretcher in under him and think about the next step. I'd like to get away as soon as possible.'

He said it softly, but a sense of urgency came through

to her. Then, as she slipped the cervical collar into place and fastened it, she saw a dark contusion on the man's skull, slightly behind and above his right ear. His eyes were closed so she couldn't check his pupils, but Jack must suspect a possible haematoma for him to risk moving the man before more convenient transport arrived on the scene.

'We'll try to take the two bikes back in tandem,' he announced. 'Adam, you'll drive one and I'll sit on the back and hold one end of the stretcher, while Christa drives the second bike and Michael holds the other end.'

It's impossible, Christa wanted to shout, but Adam's eyes were fixed on her and she knew that she couldn't let him see her doubts.

'We'll leave the big pack here, and trust to the policeman from Carlisle to get it back to us somehow,' Jack decreed, and he lifted the drug bag and handed it to Christa, then crossed to where the bikes were parked to examine them.

'If we sit right back we should be able to rest the stretcher on one thigh,' he said to Michael, who had joined him in contemplation of the problem.

'The American Indians used to drag injured or elderly people on a sled behind a horse,' Michael said, frowning as he tried to picture the procedure Jack had suggested.

'He's got a fractured pelvis and possible spinal injuries so we can't bump him back to the camp behind one of the bikes,' Jack objected.

'No, but we might be able to do it one behind the other, rather than trying to keep the two bikes side by side. Say you drive the front bike, and we attach the stretcher firmly to this tray at the back. Christa can sit back to back with you, and keep an eye on things, steadying the stretcher. We fit the other end of the stretcher to these thingummies

here—' He pointed to a metal brace across the mudguard
of one of the other bikes, then tugged at it to test its
strength.

'If Adam drives I can reach around him and hold onto
it as well to provide an extra safeguard. I could even take
the pack on my back—save leaving it.'

Christa watched as Jack considered the problem.

'It's damned risky either way, but even if we get halfway
back before a vehicle arrives it would be a help. Let's get
a couple of straps out of the pack and see if it's possible.'

The hardest part, she realised later as they set off at a
snail's pace towards the camp and the plane, had been
keeping the bikes upright while the stretcher was attached.
She was pleased that Warren had succumbed to the painkil-
ling injection Jack had given him. Seeing how they
intended transporting him would have been enough to
bring on heart failure!

It took an hour, and by the time they came in sight of
the plane Christa's hands felt as if they were moulded to
the stretcher and her arms and shoulders ached with the
strain of trying to steady it over the worst of the bumps.

Two heavy-duty vehicles indicated that more help had
arrived. She saw a woman run from the caravan as their
strange procession drew near, then a man in the wide-
brimmed hat of the outback policeman appeared behind
her. They both reached out to hold the stretcher when the
bikes stopped moving.

'We'd just read your note,' the woman said to Adam,
but Christa could see the pain in her face as she looked
down at her injured husband.

'He's a fine boy you have here,' Jack said, taking the
weight of the stretcher from her. She looked up, then
moved away from the man she so obviously loved to take
her son into her arms.

'Don't forget the sandwiches,' he said gruffly to Christa when a fresh bout of tears had been hidden against his mother's dress.

'Could we take them with us?' she asked. 'If we eat them on the plane we'll be able to get your dad to hospital sooner.'

She walked towards the caravan with him, knowing that Jack would want to speak to his mother while Michael and the policeman loaded the stretcher onto the plane.

The sandwiches were on a plate, with a teatowel thrown over them to protect them from opportunist flies. Thick wedges of bread had been spread with butter and a brightly coloured jam which was undoubtedly Adam's favourite. There were enough to feed a small army.

'They look great,' Christa told him, trying not to think of him sawing through the bread and spreading it with jam while he tried to keep panic at bay. 'How about you keep some for yourself and your mother and the police-man, and I'll wrap up enough for us to eat on the plane?'

Would Mrs Fielding and Adam come to town with them? she wondered, looking around at the well-equipped camp-site they would have to leave unattended.

'I'll pack up here and lock everything up, and should be able to leave tonight.' The woman came bustling in, answering the question. 'Jack says there's nothing we can do at the moment and, if we get away before dark, we should be in town before morning.'

Adam wrapped half the sandwiches in plastic wrap, and handed them to Christa. She said goodbye to both of them, but Mrs Fielding's mind was already on the tasks she had ahead of her. The woman followed her out towards the plane.

'Don!' she called, obviously to the policeman. 'Could you run out to the bore and bring Warren's bike back for me? Adam and I will load everything into the big trailer and lock it up. If you could keep an eye on things when you're out this way I'd be grateful.'

With a final wave to Adam Christa climbed into the plane, marvelling at the resourcefulness of these outback people. Warren's injuries could keep him in hospital for months, and this woman was calmly locking up their life's possessions and following him to town—as willingly as she must have followed him into these isolated areas of the bush when she'd agreed to marry him.

That was love! she decided. She dropped Adam's sandwiches onto the bag that contained the ones she'd packed and, picking up a blank patient file, she strapped herself into her seat while Jack connected Warren to the monitor and slipped an oxygen mask into place.

As soon as they were airborne Jack began his second, and more thorough, assessment, dictating his findings to Christa—who jotted them on to the file.

When he finished and moved across to a seat Christa took a packet of sandwiches and a paper cup of juice through to Michael, and offered the same to Jack.

He ate absent-mindedly, then turned in his seat and said quietly, 'I think Warren must have hit one of the cross-struts as he fell. There's a lot of swelling around the head wound, but I think there's a compressed fracture beneath it.'

Christa nodded. That explained why they had hurried the transfer back to the plane. A depressed fracture could required surgery to repair dural lacerations or prevent cerebral herniation. Other complications, like haematomas and intracranial infections, made hospital admission a necessity. She closed her eyes, and and said a silent prayer that Adam's father would recover. The boy deserved that much.

'Shall I run you home?' Jack asked as they watched the ambulance drive away into the gathering dusk.

Had he seen her arrive with Andrew, or merely noticed that her car was missing from the staff parking area?

'Yes, please,' she said meekly, but she wondered what this quiet man was thinking. Did he concern himself at all with staff relationships—apart from the effect they might have on the smooth running of the Base? Was he even aware of what went on beyond the narrow confines of his work?

He spoke of Warren as they drove home, telling Christa of a day he'd once spent with him when a plane had had engine trouble and they'd been grounded until a replacement could be flown in.

'He searched for water holding two bits of wire in his hands and—if it had been anyone else but him—I'd have sworn he was manipulating them.'

'Did you try it?' she asked, keeping up her end of the conversation, although her stomach was now churning with apprehension and her mind was too tired to think.

Jack turned to her and grinned.

'I did, and they twitched across each other in the exact same place, but I still can't believe it's anything more than mumbo-jumbo.'

'That's a scientific mind for you,' she said lightly. 'Refusing to accept something for which you have no logical explanation.'

And, as she said the words, she knew that they were true of herself as well. Part of her present confusion arose from the fact that she couldn't understand what was happening between herself and Andrew. Nor could she find a logical reason why it should be happening now!

And as for what she was going to do about it? Well, that was as unanswerable as the 'how water divining works' question Jack had come up against.

'Here you are,' Jack announced, and she realised that she was home. Already! She'd had no time at all to think! She sat there, reluctant to leave the security of the car.

'See you tomorrow,' Jack said, oblivious to her procrastination. 'Andrew's coming in to talk about Caltura. I think Leonie spoke to you about accompanying the eye specialist out there on Tuesday and staying on with him for the week.'

Tuesday! Staying on for the week! The words shrieked through her mind, and suspicion flared.

No! she told herself as she pushed the car door open and clambered out. She bent to say goodbye to Jack, then watched him drive away.

Definitely not! she affirmed silently. Andrew wouldn't have set himself to seduce someone for the convenience of a bed-mate for the few extra nights I'll be at Caltura and a fortnightly release of sexual energy thereafter!

The timing was coincidental, she told herself, and walked towards her house, the weariness she knew she should be feeling kept at bay by a tingling apprehension.

CHAPTER FOUR

ANDREW rose from a chair on her enclosed verandah as Christa walked up the stairs.

'Are you sure you enjoy this job?' he asked, his voice betraying an amused sympathy, while his gaze roved over her dusty, tear-smudged clothes and up to her face—which she knew would show signs of the strain she was feeling.

'Sometimes I wonder,' she replied, taking her own inventory. Showered and freshly shaven, he smelt faintly of the citrus leaves she used to crush in her hand as a child then sniff to catch the sharp, intoxicating tang.

The scent of aftershave intensified and, somehow, she was standing in his arms, drawing strength from the warmth of his body, while her weariness drained away. His fingers massaged her back, easing the tension from her shoulders as they worked to relax the tight muscles. Then one hand held her close while the other crept up, rubbing at her scalp with a magical touch—seeking out the sore places and soothing them with gentle pressure, lifting her thick, bobbed, gritty hair to coax blood back to her skin.

'I've made fettuccini with a light tomato and basil sauce,' he murmured, holding her against his rock-hard body. 'Do you feel up to eating something before you tumble into bed?'

Fettuccini with a light tomato and basil sauce? Her mouth was already watering—again her senses reacting before her brain could make the decision.

'Breakfast I'll accept,' she said, pushing her body away

from his before it started getting ideas of its own. 'Most
men can cook bacon and obviously some can scramble
eggs—but pasta sauces? Were you a chef in your other
life—before you blew into Caltura like a cyclonic wind?'

There was space between them but she was held a willing captive within the circle of his arms, and he looked
down into her face—from his six feet to her five
feet seven!

His eyes were grave and she realised that they were
darker at these times, lightening to silver when he laughed
or teased her.

'I enjoy cooking,' he said, and a nudge of caution
reminded her that this wasn't the first time he hadn't—
quite—answered her question. She considered pursuing it
but the electrical impulses of his body were beginning to
penetrate her shield of tiredness, causing complications
that she knew she couldn't handle in her present state of
near-exhaustion.

'Well, it sounds wonderful,' she said. She shifted reluctantly away from him. 'I'll just remove several tons of
dirt from my person and be right with you.'

His lowered his arms and looked her up and down, then
wrinkled his nose in mock distaste while his lips teased
into a grin.

'You do look as if you've crawled through a container
of bull-dust—and to think I hugged you!'

'Look at yourself!' she retorted. 'Hugging me, as you
put it, didn't do much for your snappy outfit either.'

He examined the dust streaks on his pale blue shirt, and
his smile widened.

'I'd better have a shower too,' he murmured, challenging her with a glint of blatant sexuality dancing in his
eyes. For a moment she was tempted, and the blazing heat
of desire flooded the most intimate parts of her body. Too

far, too fast, her common sense cautioned.

'There are two showers in this house,' she pointed out, and swept away before an image of their naked bodies, slick with cascading jets of water, could destroy what was left of her equilibrium.

She stepped, fully clothed, into the shower, knowing that if she took off her clothes first the fine, dry dust would cover every surface of the bathroom and hide away in corners for weeks. The water flowed over her, running in brown rivulets down her legs and swirling muddily into the drain hole.

The heat loosened her taut muscles and she peeled off her wet clothes, dumping them in a heap in one corner of the shower-tray before she shampooed her hair and soaped her body—glorying in the delight of being really clean at last.

She was tempted to remain under the water for as long as possible, but she could feel tiredness creeping back into her legs and knew that her body would insist on sleep before long.

She dried herself, sniffing at her towel. It smelt clean and fresh, although she knew she'd used it this morning. Had her house guest done the washing while she was away? She looked around and saw a second towel, neatly folded, hung across the other rail, and the fledgling shadow of uncertainty she kept trying to ignore grew a little larger.

Does it matter? she asked herself, pulling on her white towelling robe and wrapping the dry towel turban-style around her wet hair.

Only if he's trying to ingratiate himself with you for some reason of his own, the shadow told her. She slathered cream onto her face and arms, before leaving the safety of the bathroom to face him once again. Don't fall for all this domesticated stuff! it added warningly.

The food smelled wonderful and she forgot the warning and weakly accepted his administrations, letting him lead her to a chair and place the bowl of tender pasta with its bright splash of delicate sauce in front of her.

He moved across to the oven, as if the kitchen were his natural domain, and lifted out a wicker basket of chunky bread, brownly crisp at the edges and soft with butter and assorted fresh herbs in the middle. The aroma teased at her palate and she knew that the weak defences her doubts had erected were already crumbling into nothingness.

'Freshly grated Parmesan,' he offered, taking a seat opposite her and pushing a small bowl, piled high with yellow shreds of cheese, towards her.

She sprinkled cheese on the pasta, accepted a piece of herb bread and tried the meal, feeling a warm glow of contentment as the subtle flavours slid across her taste buds.

'It certainly beats the sandwiches I brought home,' she said, looking up and smiling at him. 'They're in my bag— I couldn't eat them all, or leave them or throw them away.'

He raised one eyebrow and, as she ate—silently acknowledging his mastery at tantalising all her senses— she told him about Adam.

'He sounds like the boy I'd like my son to be,' he said, and shock thudded through her.

Her head jerked up and she caught him watching her intently, as if gauging her reaction to his words.

'Your son?' she repeated weakly. He'd been putting so much effort into this seduction because he was a married man! Disappointment soured the taste of the food, and she pushed her plate away.

'He's only seven and, at the moment, so influenced by his mother—so protective of her—he'll barely speak to me.'

Emotion crisped the words, and she felt his pain sear through her.

Married men used a woman's sympathy for their own ends, the inner voice reminded her.

'He lives in Melbourne?' she asked, hoping that she sounded politely interested. Her shock, and her sorrow for him, were hidden beneath the words.

He nodded.

'I went down to visit him, and to apply to the family court for more access. When I first came north the court agreed with my wife that it was too far for him to travel alone and access should be restricted to times when I could get to Melbourne, but I've been thinking of buying a light plane and, that way, I could fly down and collect him.'

Christa barely heard the explanation, her mind stumbling into chaos over the fact that he'd said 'my wife'— not 'my ex-wife'! But family court—and access? Didn't that mean a divorce had taken place?

'And how often have you been down there?' Her stomach churned, but convention dictated that she carried on as if this were a perfectly normal conversation. Which it should have been, if you considered that—apart from one hug—nothing had happened between them—not even a kiss!

'I thought I'd be able to make it once a month, but you know how busy I've been. Last week was the first. . .'

His voice trailed away—the first intimation she had ever had that Andrew Walsh might, at times, feel a little of the uncertainty which most normal human beings experienced.

Then she thought of his meeting with his son—with the little boy who wouldn't speak to him—and her heart ached with an urge to reach out and comfort him.

'I'll wash the dishes, seeing you cooked,' she said, push-

ing back her chair and standing up so quickly that her knee
banged against the table. An involuntary gasp escaped her
and she bent to rub it, but Andrew was lost in his own pain.

She cleared the table, trying to ignore the conflict raging
inside her.

'I think I'll have to go to bed.' The dishes were put
away, all traces of the meal had been removed, and still
Andrew sat in silence. 'It's been a long day. Could I get
you a coffee? Would you like a drink? There's a bottle of
whisky somewhere—a gift from a grateful patient.'

He turned towards her—slowly, like a man awakening
from a dream. For a moment he looked at her blankly, as
if he couldn't remember who she was or what she was
doing in his presence, then he smiled.

'Thank you, but, no!' he said, and the zapping electricity
that had been arcing in the air between them for the last
twenty-four hours was gone. Killed by thoughts of his
wife? Was he still in love with her?

'Then I'll say goodnight. See you in the morning.'
Christa spoke briskly, telling herself that she should be
pleased, not sorry—thankful that she didn't have to con-
tend with his sexual attraction when she lacked the energy
to do credit to the battle.

But disillusionment ripped through her body. He could
turn his sexuality on and off at will! And *that* was not a
happy thought to take to bed.

She half woke at times during the night, aware of his
presence in the house as one was aware of an approaching
storm. Then, perversely, sleep would claim her, as if the
fact that he was nearby was reassuring in some way.

At five she woke and knew that she wouldn't sleep
again. It was still dark, but by the time she'd dressed and
put on her socks and joggers the darkness had faded to
the pearly luminescence of dawn.

Creeping out of the house, she whistled to Wally then followed his cavorting progress out of the yard and down towards the beach where she jogged each morning. Fresh, clean, salt-laden air flooded her lungs, and well-being surged through her. Today was a working day, and she could escape to the office. She would bury herself in piles of paperwork to chase away the last vestiges of hormonal excitement Andrew had—perhaps unknowingly—aroused.

The house was empty when she returned—and the air felt strangely heavy with his absence. A note said that he had some business to attend to, thanked her for her hospitality and added that he'd catch up with her at the Base later.

'Just as well,' she told Wally, setting out food and fresh water for him in the shade beneath the house. 'I've told you before—men only complicate things.'

He wagged his tail and looked up earnestly into her face as if he sensed a shift in her mood.

'You don't count,' she told him, pulling at his ears. 'You're still a pup! And remind me to speak to Bobbie next door about your food and exercise while I'm away.'

His eyes were warm and steady, as if he understood every word she said, and his unspoken devotion comforted her—although she didn't know why she should need comforting.

She dressed for work, while Andrew's presence hovered around her like the cloud of perfume left by some women as they passed by in the street. She sniffed the air, thinking that it might be the lemony smell of his aftershave lingering on to give her body ideas—but could not detect it.

'Get to work,' she told herself, annoyed that her thoughts were constantly turning towards him and that more dangerous fantasies persisted within the secret places of her body.

'So, all present and correct—apart from one pair of honeymooners.'

Jack surveyed his staff with a pleased smile and Christa, looking around the table, saw Peter's knee press against Katie's and watched the colour fluctuate in her cheeks. For a split second she felt a shaft of pure envy, then Jack was saying something about welcomes and all the others were looking towards the door.

Andrew walked forward and pulled up a chair. Although Susan and Sally sat between them Christa could feel her awareness of him as acutely as if he were touching her.

'Seeing Andrew is able to join us, we'll hurry through the usual housekeeping things then get on to Caltura,' Jack suggested, turning to Eddie first to ask about rosters and any problems he might be expecting with Allysha away.

'As long as she's back before Michael's wife has the baby we should be right,' Eddie told him. Christa turned to Jack, pleased to find something—apart from Andrew— to occupy her thoughts. They were all concerned over Melissa Ward's pregnancy, which had been unstable from the beginning. Now that she was getting closer to full term the likelihood of pre-eclampsia or full-blown eclampsia increased.

'We could put on a contract pilot for a few months if you want to keep yourself free to take Michael's flights in an emergency,' Leonie suggested. 'Financially we're well off at the moment, thanks to the generous donations we received during the Queen of the Outback Quest.'

Christa saw Katie blush again—she'd been their Quest

entrant—then turn to smile at the base manager. A
patient's father, Alessandro Solano, had boosted the
money raised with a substantial cheque. Had Leonie talked
him into it?

She was considering all the internal politics at play when
she heard her name mentioned, and decided that she'd
better listen to what was being said.

'I know you've agreed to Christa staying out at Caltura
this week to assist the eye specialist,' Andrew was saying,
'but what the settlement needs is a trained sister there full
time. I've done what I can, learning as I went along and
setting up the hospital. Your extra visits, Jack, have got
us back on track as far as general health is concerned, but
the population's big enough to warrant a nurse.'

He sounded tetchy, as if frustrated to find a problem
that he couldn't solve—immediately!

'But we can't provide that person,' Jack pointed out.
'It's up to the community to advertise and employ someone. We've worked with the Health Department before,
vetting health workers for Caltura, and would be glad to
do interviews for you if you advertise for a nursing sister,
but Caltura's different in some way. They haven't been
able to hold on to health workers, so how are they going
to manage to attract and keep a nurse?'

'It's because of their wanting to return to some of their
tribal beliefs,' Susan interjected. 'They were among the
first Aboriginal people "westernised"—for want of a better
word—by missionaries. Then they had other outsiders
coming in—schoolteachers at first and then when the lands
were handed back to the people, they had government
officials arriving to tell them how to run things.'

'I remember when that happened,' Eddie added. 'The
people seemed to lose heart and half the population shifted
to town, only going back to the settlement when they ran

out of money or were in trouble with the law. It got so
bad that four years ago. . .' he turned questioningly to
Susan for confirmation '. . .the elders kicked out everyone
but tribally related people, and decided they would run
things on their own. Outsiders can visit, but they can't
stay longer than is absolutely necessary.'

Christa turned towards Andrew, wondering how much
of this he knew.

'That policy remains in place,' he confirmed. 'I've
arranged for two local people—a sister and brother—to
live here in town while they train as nurse-aides, and so far
have one young woman interested in undertaking nursing
training when she finishes her secondary schooling at the
end of the year—but it will be five years before she's
qualified to return.'

'*If* she wants to return,' Susan warned, and Andrew
grinned and shrugged. Somehow he didn't seem as
perturbed as he should have been.

'Why are they so paranoid about outsiders?' Jane, the
third nursing sister, asked. 'I mean, the other settlements
have European teachers and some places have white
nursing staff.'

Somewhere in the air another question hovered, Christa
thought—the unasked, And who are you that you're
accepted? Then Andrew was speaking again, and she set
aside this mystery of his past and concentrated on what
he was saying.

'I think things had become so bad at Caltura that going
back to basics was the only way the elders could see to
stop the rot. In pre-European days, the Aboriginals had
well-defined rules that governed all their behaviour.'

He was sketching out his story in the air and, as Christa
watched the movement of his fingers, she had to remind
herself she was supposed to be thinking about his words

and not how those fingers might feel moving on her skin.

'Young people knew how they should treat their mother-in-law, for example, or their older brother or sister. They knew the formalities for greeting and caring for other clansmen from within their tribe and visitors from other tribes on feast days or great gatherings. They had rules governing their marriages, the protection of their young women, the burial of their dead—everything.

'When Europeans came they were taught new rules—religious ones at first, then governmental regulations that were meaningless to their way of life—and the old behaviours were lost. The young people drifted away and, without the guidance they needed, usually found themselves in trouble.'

'So what's happening at Caltura at the moment is a cultural experiment?' Jack asked, his eyes gleaming with interest in the concept.

'You could say that!' Andrew said drily. 'A cultural experiment that was tottering towards disintegration when I arrived. Going back to the past for guidance is one thing, but the people of Caltura are living in the present day and age. They need the material things of this world, like food and clothes, and they want the technological excitements—motorbikes, electricity, video players and stereos! In fact, they need money as well.'

'Which is why you're working so hard to build up the cattle station?' Christa knew that he spent most of his time working with the men at the out-station.

'Exactly!' He leaned forward to smile at her, and she tried to pretend that this subtle rearrangement of facial muscles hadn't affected her in the slightest. 'Caltura was once one of the best beef-producing properties in the district, and there's no reason why it shouldn't be again. I am trying to prove they can have it both ways—regulating their private and social lives in the old way, but at the same time working towards commercial success. It can be done without compromising their efforts to retain their cultural heritage if we organise things properly.'

'Boy, have you taken on a lifelong challenge,' Eddie remarked, and the other staff all chuckled.

But Christa had heard the passion in Andrew's voice, and sensed the fire that was driving him along this path.

'I'm glad we've talked about this,' Jack said, his voice deep with his unspoken admiration for their visitor. 'We will certainly do anything we can to help you and the elders of the settlement achieve your dreams, and it might also make us more sensitive to our patients in other settlements. But a permanent nursing sister is something you'll have to find for yourself.'

He turned to look at Christa.

'Now, are you organised to go tomorrow? As you all know, the specialist who went out there when Matt Laurant first found the trachoma problem wanted follow-up work done after the three months of daily systemic treatment. He also wanted someone to assess the scar tissue caused by the trachoma follicles of those most badly affected, and decide if more people will require surgery to repair their eyelids.

'This new specialist in town, Ned Cummings, has volunteered his time. All he's asking is that we provide him with a nurse.'

'I'll sort through our copies of the patient files today,' Christa assured him. 'The details of the first team's work will be noted on each individual's file. Are we including those people who came into town for surgery earlier and those who are waiting for corneal implants?'

'Have Ned check them all, Christa and, if you've time,

you might run eye tests on the kids. Are they all meeting
for school lessons again?'

Jack switched his attention back to Andrew, and Christa
finished making entries in her notebook. If she could keep
busy for the time she was at Caltura. . .

The meeting moved on to quick follow-up reports on
patients the Service had brought to town recently, finishing
with an encouraging bulletin on Warren Fielding. Leonie
added a stern reminder about requisition forms and they
broke up, Katie turning towards the radio while Peter
fielded a phone call.

Sally left the room first, always keen to get on with the
filing they knew could multiply if left undone for any
length of time. Leonie, Jack and Eddie headed towards
Leonie's office and Jane crossed to the shelves of reference
books, riffling through the recent medical magazines in
search of some information.

Which leaves me and Andrew, Christa thought.

'Would you like a coffee?' she asked him, uncertain
what he intended doing for the rest of the day—and where
he intended spending the night.

'I'd love one,' he said, standing up and stretching then
following her towards the staff kitchen. 'You must be
pleased young Adam's father is doing so well.'

Warmed by his remembering a little thing like the boy's
name, she turned and smiled and was hit by the full force
of his magnetic appeal—again!

She swung hurriedly away, knowing that she wasn't
equipped to deal with this sexual tug-of-war in her own
workplace, and reached up to pull mugs and coffee out of
the cupboard.

'I'm sorry I missed you this morning. I take Wally for
a run before breakfast.'

She spoke to break the silence, but the words didn't

chase away the tantalising impulses of desire which his body seemed to be transmitting.

'I had arranged to meet Charlie and Wanda on the Esplanade for breakfast,' he explained in turn. 'They are the brother and sister from Caltura who are training as aides, and they'd been away for the weekend so a meeting before they started work seemed best,' he explained.

She turned to put the two mugs of coffee on the table and waved her hand towards the milk and sugar, wondering what she could talk about next.

'Christa!'

She looked up and saw his steady gaze fixed on her face. The impulses quickened and her breathing slowed. How could this happen—that one man could make her pulses race while others had as little physical impact on her as her female friends and colleagues?

'I'm going to stay with them tonight,' he explained, while her breathlessness made her chest ache. His eyes held hers, conveying messages even more potent than those generated by his body. 'Yesterday you said you wanted time to think,' he added, his voice so low and gravelly that she seemed to feel it scrape against her spine. 'Then work intruded, and last night you were so tired. . .'

'I don't know what you're asking,' she managed to utter through lips as dry as tinder.

He moved closer and his voice softened as he murmured, 'Don't you, Christa?' while his presence bombarded her with sensual temptation.

Don't give in to it, the shadow of doubt warned, and she strained against the hunger that was consuming her.

'No, I don't!' she said, straightening up, determined to regain some control over a situation that was running wild. She met his gaze defiantly, and, while her heart hammered and her body pulsed with the excitement he had called into existence, she said the words that she knew had to be said for her own peace of mind—her own sanity.

'You spoke of your wife. Is this to be an extra-marital affair? Is that what you want? Someone to satisfy your libido once a fortnight when I'm at Caltura or at times when you're passing through town?'

She didn't add—because I don't think I could handle that. Didn't tell him that she suspected that once he'd even so much as kissed her she would be bonded to him for life!

His face grew pale, she saw his eyes darken and, for an instant, she felt an unreasonable tremor of fear.

'Do you think I would offer you that?' he growled. 'Do you think I respect you so little that I would demean you in that way? I have watched you work; seen your empathy with others; learnt to admire you as a person—'

He paused as if the enormity of her misunderstanding had left him speechless.

'Well, what was I supposed to think? We've known each other long enough—why now? Why me?' She spoke angrily, feeling uncomfortable—and somehow guilty—because she'd upset him.

'Why you? Why now?' he murmured, and moved a step closer.

Christa felt the force of his attraction battering at her body. He *could* turn it on and off at will!

She stepped back and read his reaction in a stiffening of his body. Turning away from him, she dug into the sugar with a teaspoon as if the answer to her perturbation might be buried beneath the crystals.

'I thought we might explore the attraction that exists between us, certainly, and give each other some physical pleasure.'

She shivered in response and looked up at him again. The grey eyes, almost black with suppressed anger, bored into hers. 'But my intentions were honourable, Christa. I was thinking of marriage ahead for us both. My divorce will be final in a month. Do you need that long to think?'

He swept out of the room, leaving her speechless. She was overwhelmingly aware that she'd offended him, and even more aware of her own deep sense of loss.

She wanted to run after him—to apologise—then the full impact of his final words hit her, and she sank into a chair and ran her hands through her hair, massaging her scalp as if the physical effort would help her brain assimilate their meaning.

Marriage? He was thinking that far ahead? Marriage—before they'd even kissed? Sexual compatibility and marriage—Daniel's excuse! Had love ceased to exist? Was it no longer a prerequisite for marriage?

She'd been looking for reassurance that there might be something more to this sudden interest than sex—maybe a hint of feeling; a prelude to love—but she certainly hadn't thought as far as marriage. Nor had she thought as prosaically! As cold-bloodedly?

She shook her head in helpless confusion, but at the same time felt a tiny trickle of excitement start up along her skin. Were marriage and Andrew so diametrically opposed that she couldn't even consider it?

But he's gone, she reminded herself. There's no point in thinking about it.

She tipped the two cups of coffee down the sink and walked slowly back to her desk, pausing on the way to pull the Caltura files out of the cabinet. She sorted through them, determined to concentrate on her work. That way she could exclude Andrew Walsh from her thoughts.

Six patients had been brought from Caltura to town for surgery immediately after the first assessment, and another twenty-five had been listed for follow-up examination after treatment.

She knew most of them because, since Andrew had taken on the role of health worker at the settlement, he had made himself responsible for seeing people kept their appointments when the Flying Doctor visited.

'How many of the serious cases have diabetes?' Jack's voice interrupted thoughts that were veering dangerously away from the files!

'I haven't checked that out,' she told him as he perched on one corner of her desk. 'Are you thinking some of the blindness could be caused by diabetic retinopathy?'

'I know of a couple of cases. On my first visit I think I marked the diabetic cases with a red flash.' He pulled a file towards him and opened it, then pointed to the red mark. 'See, I thought I remembered doing that. I had an idea about getting someone to feed the information into the computer and trying to trace family relationships, but we've been so busy I haven't got around to organising it.'

'Well, it will make my job easier,' Christa told him. 'It gives me a way to classify the patients. If I put the people with diabetes first when I draw up the appointment lists it should make things simpler for Dr Cummings.'

Jack smiled and nodded.

'And have you worked out how you're going to get these people to appointments?' he asked. 'Remember, Andrew's over here at the moment so he won't be chasing them up.'

As if I could forget! Christa thought.

'Well, tomorrow is a normal clinic day,' she pointed out, 'and Andrew assured us last visit that he had a deputy who would bring the people in if he was ever away from Caltura.'

She smiled at Jack, pleased that she'd been able to say Andrew's name without stammering.

'If you could include the women who will come for pregnancy checks with me on your patient list I could take Dr Cummings over to the school and do eye tests on the kids.'

'That will be a novel experience for him—he's an Englishman, you know,' Jack interjected, and Christa smiled, imagining the man squatting in the dirt beneath the rough bark and branch shelter that constituted 'the school'.

Part of Caltura's 'back to basics' approach had been to remove the children from the 'western' schoolhouse and conduct all school work, whether formalised School of the Air lessons or instruction in the old ways and customs, outside.

'And you'll set up his appointments for the following day, then surgery on the Thursday,' Jack continued, his voice echoing his satisfaction with the arrangements. 'Ned's flying back on Friday—Eddie has arranged a light plane to collect him. Are you happy to stay on to care for the surgical patients? It means giving up your weekend!'

'What a tragedy!' Christa said lightly, while her nerves played havoc with her stomach. 'Anyway, by Sunday all the patients should have been released. I'll get more rest out there on Sunday than I did at home yesterday,' she reminded him.

But would she? Was Andrew serious when he said that she had a month to think about things? Would he hide himself away over at the cattle property while she was at Caltura?

Jack was chatting on, reliving their adventurous ride, but her thoughts had drifted away—back to Andrew's furious departure from the kitchen.

How was she to have known what he was thinking? In her limited experience, marriage was the last thing in most men's minds when they began to woo a woman. With the exception of Daniel, of course! He'd used the assumption of their future marriage to convince her that she should consent to his love-making, pointing out that their marriage wouldn't work if they weren't compatible. The way he'd explained it, it had been her duty to allow him to seduce her and she, foolish virgin that she'd been, had believed him.

She hid the shudder that rippled through her at the memory, and murmured something meaningless to Jack as he moved away from her desk. For nine years she'd managed to put aside those memories of Daniel. Would she have to dig them up again and face that particular failure before she could go on with her life? Before she could even consider Andrew's strange declaration?

CHAPTER FIVE

THE names seemed to leap out at her as Christa sorted through the files. Charlie and Wanda, he had said, and here was Charlie Renmako and a Wanda with the same surname. A notation—in her own handwriting—at the bottom of the file gave their current address in Rainbow Bay.

She worked through the morning, trying to ignore the argument that was raging within her. She had upset Andrew with her brash supposition and she knew that she would feel uncomfortable about that until she saw him again—and apologised.

On the other hand, the information on the files was privileged and she was aware, without doubt, that it would be wrong to use it for personal reasons. Unethically, dismissably wrong, her conscience reminded her.

As she typed up the list of appointments for Dr Cummings she wondered if she could make the list a work-related excuse. She imagined the conversation when she arrived on the Renmakos' doorstep.

'I just dropped by to give this list to Andrew.'

'Oh, he's in, is he? Could I see him?'

'I'm sorry I misjudged you. I can't imagine why I thought you had only sex in mind!'

It sounded so ridiculous that she groaned aloud, halting Sally—who was walking past with a tray of steaming coffee-mugs.

'You OK?' she asked, and Christa nodded. The last thing she needed was to draw attention to her confusion.

'I'll take this coffee through to the office, and come back. Maybe I can give you a hand.'

'Thanks, but I'll manage,' Christa assured her and then, more to change the subject than for any other reason, she asked, 'Is Leonie entertaining someone important?' and nodded at the tray.

Sally shook her head.

'She's talking to Jack and Andrew Walsh,' she explained. 'And isn't he a dishy bloke?'

Isn't he just? Christa thought gloomily as Sally went on her way. The knowledge that Andrew was still in the building—that he hadn't stormed away—had sent her heartbeat into a frenzy. From her vantage point in the open-plan office space she would see him when he emerged from Leonie's office.

She could give him the lists and—? Ask him to dinner! The thought came like a revelation from on high! After all, he'd cooked twice for her—shouldn't she return the favour?

She finished typing the appointment lists, her fingers flying across the keys, then pulled out a nursing manual to read up on post-operative care for ophthalmology patients. The thought of returning to something like 'ward' nursing excited her, even if it was only for a few days.

'Peace?'

His voice startled her and she looked up and frowned. So much for keeping an eye out for him to emerge!

'Peace?' she repeated, her mind bogged down in the effects of sensory deprivation on her potential patients.

'I'm sorry I blew up earlier,' he said softly, looking down at her with his eyes shadowed by his long, dark lashes so that she couldn't see the expression in them or judge their colour! 'I'm sorry I was so—touchy?'

She tried to smile, but her heart was pounding furiously

and she was using all her available energy to control it.

'Would you like to come to dinner?' She heard the rehearsed invitation tripping off her lips.

'I'm sorry, I can't,' he explained. 'I've arranged to meet a fellow about some business, but I'll see you at the airport in the morning. We'll have other times, Christa.'

She felt the implications of his words strike sparks along her nerves, but she couldn't think of anything to say. He reached out and touched her lightly on the cheek then walked away, leaving her feeling restless and uncertain.

And still holding the appointment list she'd typed for him!

They met in the soft, rosy light of dawn. Ned Cummings, the ophthalmologist, was in his early thirties and enthusiastic about the project he was about to undertake. He was talking to Andrew, who lifted a hand to her in greeting as she walked past towards the hangar to collect the equipment they would need.

'All set for your stay in the bush?' Jack asked.

'Looking forward to it,' she replied, although the butterflies in her stomach gave the lie to the words.

Five minutes later they were on their way. The newcomer had been given the copilot's seat, and Jack was in the seat behind the pilot. For a moment Christa dithered, wondering if it was better to have Andrew behind her and take all the force of his presence on her back or in front where she'd be able to see him during the sixty-minute flight.

He solved that problem by slipping into the seat behind Jack, snapping his seat belt into place then turning around to smile at her as she took the seat behind him.

The smile made him look young and boyish, and excitement gleamed in eyes the colour of polished pewter. Was

it the flight? Or the fact that he was returning to Caltura?
Or something else?

The 'something else' possibility screwed her own emotional tension tighter. He turned away to reply to some
remark of Jack's and she studied the back of his head,
seeing the shine in the black hair which was cut short over
a well-shaped skull. Would it be wiry or soft, she wondered, that dark, dark hair? She longed to touch it—to test
the texture between her fingers.

Andrew sat back in his seat as the plane gathered speed
and she drew away, suddenly aware that she'd been lean-
ing embarrassingly close. She sighed frustratedly.

The way she was feeling, the sooner they—as he'd put
it—'explored the attraction between them' the better. Last
night her body had been too restless for proper sleep,
tossing and turning feverishly and filled with strange aches
that no analgesic could take away. And here she was now,
all but reaching out across the seat-back to run her fingers
through his hair!

The engines roared, lifting the plane into the sky, but
as the aircraft reached their cruising altitude and the noise
lessened he turned to her again.

'I'll give you a hand to get the kids organised for their
tests, then will have to go across to the out-station,' he
said. 'I'll try to get back to the community hall tonight. I
know the women are planning a special dinner for the eye
doctor. In fact, it's going to be a big week socially. We've
got a house-opening on Saturday night.'

'House-opening?' she repeated weakly, too bemused by
the excitement that lingered in his eyes and the force of
his teasing smile to attempt to fathom the strange term.

'You'll see,' he said, then added in a low, husky undertone, 'You'll be in Caltura on Saturday—remember?'

She shifted uneasily in her seat. How could she possibly

forget when her body seemed joined to his already by tiny, invisible wires that pulled at her flesh and tweaked her nerves to a vibrant life of their own.

'Did you give Andrew your appointment list?'

Jack had walked back down the aisle, and bent towards her as he asked the question.

Of course she hadn't! Work had been forgotten since this man she barely knew had spread his sexual web around her.

'I've got it here,' she said, reaching down into the carry-bag that held the Caltura files. She found the list and passed it forward.

'If you're busy will your new deputy hunt up these people for us?' she said, flinching as his fingers brushed against hers on the piece of paper.

'I'll see they all turn up tomorrow,' he promised, and held out the list so that Jack could read it with him.

To Christa's relief, the conversation became medical and stayed that way until they reached Caltura. Andrew helped unload the plane, stacking the equipment bags and personal belongings onto an old truck. A young man appeared on a battered off-road bike—transport Christa recognised from other visits here.

'You ready to go, Andrew?' he called, and Christa watched as Andrew shook hands with Ned and Jack then waved to Bill, who had flown them out. He came towards her, hand outstretched, and she put her hand in his and felt the gentle pressure of his fingers. Then his thumb slid across her palm, and excitement seared through her body.

'I'll be back in half an hour,' he murmured, and turned away, crossing to lift one long leg over the saddle of the bike. They roared away, dust flying behind them, and Christa once again had to consciously switch her mind back to work-related matters.

Ned Cummings had gone into culture shock, she decided after she'd shown him the makeshift hospital, led him through the community hall—where Jack was settling down to conduct his clinic—then hustled him towards the bough-shaded 'school' where Andrew waited for them.

'The people here are trying to revive some of their tribal beliefs and traditions,' Andrew explained as they paused by the 'art school'. Three men squatted on the ground, each working on a painting—meticulously arranging coloured dots, fine lines, parallel or criss-crossed, in patterns that would tell the story they were trying to depict. Beyond them women rolled strips of a native lily leaf against their thighs, making string to weave into baskets.

'That's one of the reasons they appreciate your coming out here to operate. Too often, when people go to town for medical reasons, they feel uncomfortable—displaced— which, in turn, leads to other problems.'

Ned Cummings nodded.

'Jack explained that to me,' he said, but Christa was only half-aware of his words as Andrew's presence intruded itself into every cell in her body. He led them on towards the next shaded area, where children's voices were raised in song.

'I know the tune, but not the words,' Ned remarked, and Christa smiled.

'They learn many English songs in their own language as part of their lessons, and they tell their legends in our language,' she explained. Andrew introduced Ned to the young Aboriginal teacher and the two aides who assisted him.

The children and teachers greeted Christa then sat and listened—dark eyes wide with wonder—while Ned talked about his school days, describing snow to children for whom an ice-block was a treat.

Andrew explained about the eye tests, making a joke about needing to see the fish beneath the water in the lagoon before they could spear them. A chair was found for Ned, and set up beneath an arching pepper tree.

'This is a great surgery,' he said, looking around the pale green bower. 'Now, perhaps if we pin the eye chart over there.' He pointed to a straggly eucalypt some distance away and bent over his bag, looking for a suitable chart.

The first had animals in diminishing sizes on it, and he set it to one side. The next was a standard lettered chart, which was also set aside.

'I've got something,' Christa offered, remembering a copy of another specialist's chart she'd seen as she went through the files. She rustled through her papers and found the sheet. It had birds and animals even the youngest of these children would recognise—an emu, kangaroo, frog, goanna, eagle, magpie, koala and wombat.

'Resourceful woman,' Ned said, smiling his delight.

'Well, it will do for the younger children,' Andrew told him almost gruffly, 'but you should use the letter chart for the older ones. I think they'd be most insulted if they had to read out animals like the little kids.'

Christa was surprised by his remark, and by the frown he directed towards Ned. He seemed edgy, as if he wanted to be somewhere else yet was reluctant to leave the two of them alone.

She pinned up the first chart and called to the teacher that they were ready—beginning with the young children in alphabetical order. Andrew walked across to the 'school' and marshalled the little ones into line. He chatted so easily to them, using a mixture of English and their own dialect, and—as she watched their delight in his presence—she wondered about his own son. Would love for the boy draw him back to his wife?

And that inevitably led to wondering why they had separated.

'Ready when you are.'

Ned's voice recalled her to duty. Andrew led the first child forward and knelt beside him, his arm around the skinny shoulders, while Ned examined the lad's eyes. He checked for the velvety redness on the undersides of the upper eyelids, which was the first indication of trachoma. Using an ophthalmoscope, he looked for signs of damage or injury, seeking out any potential problem. Christa wrote his findings on the relevant patient file, while Andrew encouraged the children—shy in the presence of this stranger—to name the animals on the chart.

Andrew left when the younger children had been examined, disappearing with a murmured apology and a quick smile for Christa. She and Ned worked through until lunchtime, then joined Jack in the community room where plates piled high with sandwiches and huge pots of tea awaited them.

'What do you think so far?' Jack asked, and Ned was quick to point out that the trachoma seemed to have been contained.

'I've seen signs of scar tissue in some of the children,' he said, 'but not enough to cause visual problems and no sign of any recurrence.'

'Which is always a worry,' Jack agreed. 'It's a virus that provides no ongoing immunity, so the chance of another outbreak is always on the cards.'

'But it's greatly reduced with good hygiene practices,' Ned argued. 'And, from what I've seen here, those are in place. The kids might have their lessons on a dirt floor beneath a bark roof, but they were all clean and practically glowing with health.'

'Now they are!' Jack said, but didn't elaborate on the
problems they'd had earlier in the year.

'I'm also impressed by their visual acuity. In the number
of children I've seen this morning I would have expected
at least one to be long- or short-sighted, but so far so
good. There's one youngster with a slight astigmatism,
but a lens will fix that. The child seemed quite pleased
when I talked about the possibility of glasses.'

'Maybe having glasses is a form of one-upmanship these
days,' Christa said. 'I've noticed kids are far more
accepting of them than back when I was at school.'

The conversation drifted from medical to general, then
back to medical as they returned to work. The sun had
dropped to a flaming red orb in the western sky by the
time they finished the examinations. Christa stood up and
stretched, trying to get the kinks out of her bones after
spending most of the day bent over files and using her
knees as a desk.

'Where do we sleep?' Ned asked, looking at the rough
shacks that were dotted about the place like the forgotten
props from a movie set.

'Over by the hospital,' Christa told him. 'There's a
house which was built for the schoolteacher—a proper,
government-regulation building. There are also more
modern houses at the out-station, where a number of
families live, and some newer ones up by the lagoon.' She
waved her hand towards the ramshackle shanties. 'These
are left over from the original settlement. Some of the
older people stayed on here—wanting to remain in their
own homes.'

Ned looked around with renewed interest as they walked
towards their quarters for the night. Noise and laughter
echoed from the community hall, where preparations for
the dinner were under way.

'There'll be dancing after dinner,' Christa told him.

'That's great,' he enthused. 'They seem such happy people.'

Christa agreed, but her mind was not on the conversation. The noisy engine of a motorbike had distracted her and she looked towards the track that led to the cattle property, wondering about the rider who was approaching at such speed.

It was Andrew, but he was seeking Jack—not her. A mob of cattle that had run wild in a gorge on the far boundary of the property had been rounded up and brought back to the yards. One of the young men, working them into the crush for branding, had misjudged the temper of a rogue bull and been gored in the side.

While Jack collected an equipment case Andrew issued orders. Someone was deputed to drive the truck over to the property to transport the injured stockman back to the hospital.

'I'll go with the truck,' Christa suggested. 'We can go via the airfield, collect a stretcher from the plane and let Bill know what's happening. He can get the plane ready for take-off in case Jack wants to take the patient back to town.'

'Get the Thomas pack as well,' Jack called to her, before climbing onto the bike behind Andrew.

Christa watched them ride away, then hurried to where a young man waited in the truck.

'Can I do anything?' Ned asked, following her to open the door. She shook her head.

'The house is just over there,' she said, pointing towards a shadowy building where one light burned dimly. 'Someone will have left our bags on the verandah. Why don't you have a shower and change? That way, at least one of us will be ready for the festivities.'

'But surely there won't be any festivities if someone's been badly injured?' Ned sounded bemused.

'We all have to eat,' Christa reminded him. 'If the young man's badly hurt Jack will fly him straight back to Rainbow Bay. If he can be stitched up here we'll do that but, either way, you are considered a special guest and the people will want to honour you.'

'You take it all so calmly,' he said, smiling at her. 'I guess you're right. I'll go and have a shower.'

Bill had heard of the emergency, and had the stretcher and heavy pack waiting for them.

'I'll warm the engines, and be ready to go,' he promised as he slung the equipment on to the tray.

Christa returned to the truck, climbed into the cabin and held on tightly. She knew the rough road they had to travel, and the careless ease with which the local men drove this battered old vehicle. Ten minutes later they saw the knot of people gathered by the stockyards.

'Don't go too close,' Christa warned her chauffeur. 'You don't want clouds of dust blowing into an open wound.'

The young man nodded, slowing down immediately and rolling to a standstill.

Jack knelt beside the patient while Andrew stood above him, a soft fluid bag in one hand. Christa could feel the concern that emanated from him, and longed to put a hand on his arm and whisper reassurance.

'It's a ruptured spleen and possible liver damage,' Jack explained. 'Pull out an anti-shock garment from the pack. I need to stabilise his blood pressure if I can.'

Christa dug in the pack, and produced the strange inflatable trousers they used to raise blood pressure in shock victims. Andrew passed the fluid bag to the truck driver and took them from her, following every move with foresight and intelligence. Their hands touched as she showed him how to spread them beneath the patient and strap them around both legs and pelvis. Something in the pleasure of working with him warmed her heart, and she wondered if love could spring to life so swiftly.

It can't be love, her warning shadow whispered.

'Don't inflate them around his pelvis,' Jack said. 'There could be damage there I haven't found. Could you get another fluid pack from the cold pack, Christa, and a pressure infuser? I've an IV running wide open, but on the flight more pressure will be needed because of the altitude.'

Christa hurried to find what he would need.

'Will you take him back to town?' Andrew asked, and Jack nodded.

'Christa too?'

'Not if he has a sensible relative who wants to travel with him,' Jack replied, and Christa smiled.

Jack would be actively working to reduce shock and maintain tissue balance all the way back to town, and two sets of hands were often better than one.

'He's Rod Gibson, Nellie Gibson's son,' Andrew explained. 'I'm sure she'll go with him, and she's a sensible, competent person. She will help out if necessary.'

'That's great. I know Nellie well,' Jack agreed. 'Christa has enough on her plate with Ned and the eye problems.'

Christa thought about the people she knew well at Caltura, knowing Nellie's name but unable to picture her.

'The woman who always cooks pikelets for our morning tea,' Jack reminded her, clipping the pressure infuser onto the fluid line.

Andrew was organising their departure, sending a young lad on a bike to contact Nellie then on to the schoolhouse to collect Jack's overnight bag.

'Take it to the plane,' he said, 'and tell the pilot the patient will be there within half an hour.'

He spoke quietly, but Christa could hear the habit of command in his voice and see its effect in the smart obedience of the men.

Several other stockmen had been despatched earlier and they now returned with sleeping bags which they used to pad the tray of the truck, before lifting the stretcher carefully onto it and settling beside it to hold it steady.

'Stop by Gibsons' and pick Nellie up,' Andrew said to the driver. He turned to Christa. 'I'll run you back on the bike.'

She felt a shiver crawl across her skin and moved uneasily.

'Right, we're off,' Jack said, climbing up beside his patient and taking the fluid bag from the helper. He looked down at Christa. 'Bill can fly me direct to Rosemount and Cameron River from town in the morning. Will you be OK here?'

'Of course,' she assured him, almost running to keep up as the truck began to move. 'I'm doing mostly secretarial work at the moment, and the operations on Thursday will all be under local anaesthetic so we shouldn't have any problems there.'

'Just see that you scrub down well between each one,' he reminded her, and she smiled in the darkness. He knew that she knew to do that, but he liked to be involved with every facet of the Service and it was his way of saying that he would have liked to have been there.

'Come on, I'll give you a lift over to the plane. You'll want to see them safely into the air.'

She spun around at Andrew's touch but he was already walking towards the bike, starting the engine and revving it loudly.

Give you a lift? It was one thing riding a dirt-bike on her own but a different matter when it meant sitting pressed against Andrew's body, her arms wrapped around him to prevent her being flung off!

She climbed on gingerly, wondering if she could hold onto the seat, but as the machine leapt forward she forgot her inhibitions and gripped him tightly. The heat of his body burned into hers and she smelt dust and sweat, a strange manly perfume that was more seductive than the most expensive aftershave. For a moment she was tempted to rest her cheek against his back, and dream. . .

Too far, too fast! the warning echoed, and she straightened and tried to pretend that there was nothing erotic about such artificial closeness.

The stretcher was being loaded into the plane when they arrived at the airfield, and Jack came towards them. Anxious to escape the false but weakening intimacy, Christa leapt off the bike and hurried towards him.

'How did your clinic go?' she asked, remembering other business details she hadn't checked with him. It was easy to get held up with unexpected patients or more serious concerns than were usually expected in a clinic session. 'Did you get through everyone?'

'All but a few of your women,' he admitted. 'I'm glad you mentioned that. I asked three or four of them to come back in the morning. I was going to see them at seven before the plane took off. Would you attend to that for me?'

Ahead they could see the cabin lights on in the plane and a bustle of activity as it was prepared for take-off.

'Looks like they're waiting for me,' Jack said. 'I'll let you know the arrangements for Monday. Someone will pick you up.'

He was walking away from her as he spoke, yelling

back over his shoulder. She chuckled to herself. They might all tease Jack about the way he fussed over his staff, but it was comforting at the same time.

'Happy in the Service, are you?' a suggestive voice asked, and Christa spun around to see Andrew approaching out of the darkness.

She was about to explain when she felt his arm tuck around her shoulder, and the words died on her lips as her body came alive.

They stood in the shadows and watched the plane take off, their bodies in contact all down one side so that the messages of desire and attraction had only two thin barriers of clothes to penetrate—a simple task for such powerful forces.

'We've got to go,' Christa murmured when the plane had become a memory of tail-lights in the star-filled sky.

'I know,' Andrew replied, but neither of them moved until the waiting became unbearable and Christa broke away.

Or nearly broke away!

His hand slipped from her shoulder, but grasped her wrist before she could escape. He drew her against his body, hot and hard, dust-caked and sweaty—yet providing such aching relief that her knees almost gave way.

She lifted her head to meet his kiss, pressing closer to release the heaviness in her breasts and the tingling urgency of her own arousal. His mouth took hers with a ferocity that matched her need and she responded, close to fighting him as she sought to ease the longing he'd kindled so effortlessly in a few short days.

Long and deep—a searching, seeking, soul-searing kiss that reached into Christa's heart and drew forth a tumultuous excitement to shiver through her blood and tremble in her bones.

She felt her body begin to shake and Andrew's hands moved on her back, gentling and soothing her. Then the chemistry changed between them and excitement became desire, throbbing through her with a ferocity that frightened her. She knew that he must have sensed the change, for his body tensed and his hands became more searching. Her fingers slipped into his hair, soft and silky. She tugged at it, wanting to give him pain to match her own—needing to hurt so that she could be diverted from other needs.

He whispered her name, a louder breath between them, and in the word she heard his own despairing agony that sexual hunger had aroused.

'Christa, Christa, Christa!'

Her name became a litany of longing, and she knew that she would give him anything, do anything, say anything—if only he would bring her the ecstasy and ease his body promised.

Anything?

She pushed away from him, as filled with shame as she was with longing, knowing that he could pull her down to the ground right here and now and she would willingly surrender herself to him. The thought of such a coupling ignited more flames, more shame, and she sank down onto her knees, sat on her heels and pressed her hands against her burning cheeks.

He knelt beside her and pulled her hands away.

'My fault for starting something we couldn't possibly finish at the moment,' he muttered to her, forcing her head up with his fingers so that he could look into her eyes in the silvery light of the rising moon. 'Come on, I'll walk you back to the schoolhouse.'

His voice stroked across her skin like the touch of satin, and he helped her so gently and tenderly to her feet that she wanted to cry. He kissed her once again, but this time without the fire—the kind of kiss a friend might give.

Back at the house Ned waited on the verandah, peering out into the night as if uncertain what to do or where to go next.

'I'll see you later,' Andrew whispered, and disappeared into the shadows.

'Jack's taken the injured man back to the Bay,' Christa explained. 'I've just seen them off. Give me a couple of minutes to shower and change into clean clothes, and I'll take you across to the community hall.'

She was thankful that the generated power provided only a dim light, and she hurried past Ned, knowing that her uniform would be imprinted with the shape of Andrew's body—imprinted with the dust and sweat, the smell and taste of him.

In the tiny bathroom she peered at her reflection in a tiny, fly-spotted mirror and grimaced at the flushed cheeks and wildly tousled hair. Then she looked at the dust on her patterned blouse and ran her fingers lightly over it, picking up a fleck and sniffing at it as if she might recapture the essence of the man she'd just kissed.

She felt a curious reluctance to remove her clothes. Would shedding them take him further away from her? She met her own eyes in the mirror and mocked herself for such foolishness.

She stripped off quickly and slid beneath the fitful bursts of lukewarm water, wondering, as she soaped her still-tingling body, where this strange new madness was about to lead.

Apart from Andrew's bed!

The thought of marriage had an unreality about it, clouded and obscured by the nebulous doubts that hovered deep in her subconscious.

Give it time, she told herself as she shook water out of
her hair and patted her skin dry.

She dressed quickly and escorted Ned across to the
community hall, where most of Caltura's population
waited patiently to welcome their guests. Balloons decorated the rafters and leaves and lilies from the lagoon were
ranged down the centre of the long tables, giving the otherwise bare hall a festive air.

Beyond the tables, on a raised platform, stood a set of
sequin-studded drums, a keyboard, three electric guitars—
minus their usual amplifiers—and a stand on which a
saxophone rested.

'That kind of dancing?' Ned asked, nodding towards
the band instruments. 'I thought you meant—what's the
word—corroboree?'

Christa laughed.

'I should have explained better,' she told him. 'They
keep their traditional dances for their own ceremonies,
although I'm certain, if you asked one of the older men
who will be seated near you at dinner, they would be
pleased to arrange something for you.'

'But that equipment looks expensive. Are they a
serious band?'

'Wait and judge for yourself,' Christa told him, not
adding that the group had recently toured all the capital
cities to promote their second successful album. She had
heard that they were coming home for a special occasion,
and wondered again about the 'house-opening' Andrew
had mentioned.

Dinner was a noisy affair, with conversations punctu-
ated by laughter. Christa joined in the talk, hearing an
excited update on a baby she'd delivered mid-flight and
details of what was happening to other patients she had
treated.

As older children cleared away the plates a woman she knew well rose to speak. Her name was Nancy Arnikoo, and Christa had persuaded her to fly to Rainbow Bay for treatment for endometriosis which had been making her life miserable.

Because Nancy had no family in town Christa had visited her in hospital, explaining the tests she would have to undergo and the laparoscopy the specialist would perform. After the surgical procedure Nancy had stayed at Christa's house until the gynaecologist was happy enough with her progress for her to return to Caltura.

Remembering this, Christa forced her mind away from Andrew's non-appearance and tried to concentrate on what Nancy was saying.

Within seconds her name was mentioned and she gathered, from the shy glances in her direction, that it wasn't the first time. She listened to the words, English sprinkled with their own language. Nancy was talking about relationships—a relationship, singular.

A surge of pure pleasure shafted through her body when it all became clear and, as everyone clapped, she rose to her feet and walked around the tables to Nancy, hugging her and holding her close.

She'd been adopted!

She looked around again for Andrew, wanting to share this momentous moment with him, but he hadn't arrived.

'Thank you, Nancy,' she said, knowing that it was a special honour to be taken into one of the tribal families.

'Thank you, sister,' Nancy corrected, while everyone applauded loudly. 'Now, you meet your family.'

She called out names, and all around the tables people rose and nodded towards Christa. A quick count showed that she now had twenty-something new cousins, aunts and uncles—and responsibilities she would have to learn towards each and every one of them.

'You weren't expecting that?' Ned asked as they danced to the rock band a little later.

'No way!' she told him, still smiling with delight at the unexpected honour. 'I know Jack's been adopted by a family up north, and Peter recently became a family member at Coorawalla—an island in the gulf—but me?'

She held out her hands in surprised supplication.

'They must think a lot of you,' Ned said.

'But all I do out here is the job I'm paid to do,' she pointed out, pondering the unexpectedness of it all. And wishing that Andrew was here!

Then Joe, an old man with an unpronounceable surname who she suspected was one of her new uncles, came across the dance-floor towards her.

'Radio call from Jack,' he told her. 'They arrived safely and transferred Rodney to hospital. I'm going over to the out-station now, so I'll tell Andrew. He's rigged up lights, and is trying to finish the branding while the beasts are all penned in the yards.'

And I've been feeling aggrieved that he's not here to share my new status! Christa thought, shame washing through her as she watched Joe walk away.

'Tired?' Ned asked, and she looked up to see him gazing anxiously at her.

'A bit,' she admitted. 'It's been a long day. Would you excuse me?'

She walked away, out of the hall and through the moon-lit night towards the schoolhouse.

She thought of Andrew, working by the light of bright gas lanterns, and imagined the milling cattle, the mournful cries and bellows of objection as the brand was pressed into their hides.

The first thing she'd admired about him had been his

dedication to the task he'd undertaken at Caltura. So why was she wishing that he'd been a little less dedicated tonight?

CHAPTER SIX

WITH her internal alarm set for her regular morning run with Wally, Christa woke early. She dressed quietly and slipped outside, breathing deeply in the cool dawn air. There was the perfumed piquancy of a eucalypt fire, and she looked towards the old houses to see fine, trailing wisps of smoke spiralling from where a door had once been. Many of the older people kept a small fire burning in their houses throughout the year, a relic of the time when fire had been a friendly spirit.

She turned towards the lagoon, and soon the signs of habitation disappeared. She could have been alone in the world, alone in this place of special beauty. Not wanting to approach too close for fear of offending either the spiritual or human inhabitants of the area, she leaned against the thick trunk of an old casuarina and admired the reed-edged water—lit to a tawny golden-pink as it reflected the sunrise—and the smooth perfection of the water-lily leaves that spread across it like huge dinner plates.

Had her 'adoption' made her feel more in tune with these surroundings? she wondered as the primeval beauty of the scene filled her doubtful mind and troubled body with a deep sense of peace.

Then Andrew joined her, a silent shadow appearing out of the dawn and drawing her down to sit beside him—close, but not touching. Neither spoke, for words were not needed as the miracle of the new day unfolded.

They sat for an hour while the world came to life around

them. Grey kangaroos loped past, their bounding progress
so graceful that they seemed to move to unheard music.
Beyond the lagoon black cockatoos swept into an old fig
tree, arguing raucously, then a kookaburra laughed as he
greeted the new day, and the sun rose high enough to
filter through the leaves and dapple its yellow light across
her arms.

Time to get up, to get busy, nature seemed to be saying,
and Andrew repeated the thought when he leant towards
her, kissed her cheek and murmured, 'I've got to go.'

Christa stood reluctantly, watching as he strode silently
away, then she remembered that she had patients to see
and walked briskly back to the house.

'Breakfast in the community hall at eight,' she called,
banging on Ned's door. He had stayed on at the festivities
the previous night, and must still have been sleeping. She
rinsed out her dirty clothes and hung them to dry, before
walking across to the hall.

Two women who had come for prenatal checks were
already waiting, each bearing their small samples of urine.
Was that where Andrew had disappeared to? Had he gone
to chase up their patients for today?

Christa unlocked the door that led into the examination
room she used when she was here. The hall had been
built twenty years earlier when the change from church to
government control had come into place. Two rooms had
been designed and fitted out for the Flying Doctor's visits.
Faceless bureaucrats in a far-off city had decreed that the
days of medical consultations under the trees were over.

Yet yesterday's examination of the children's eyes had
seemed so relaxed in the open-air setting! Or had Andrew's
presence made it so special? As she spread a clean sheet
on the examination couch she began to sense the feelings
of the elders who had chosen to try to draw their people

back towards some of the old ways. She called her first
patient in and began work.

'Everything's fine,' she assured the woman, Helen
Tarcutt, when her examination was completed. Helen was
thirty weeks into her first pregnancy and positively glowing with pride. 'Have you thought about where you'd like
to have the baby? Will you go up to Castleford or come
to Rainbow Bay?'

Christa saw the happiness fade from the dark eyes, and
knew that it wasn't much of a choice to offer. Castleford
was a bone-jolting three hours' drive away, and the Bay
six hours by a road that rambled over half the countryside
and was impassable in the Wet.

'Couldn't Nellie deliver it here?' the woman asked, and
Christa sighed. As far as she knew Nellie had no formal
training but she was a competent midwife, trusted by the
women at Caltura.

'You know Jack would rather you go to a hospital for
your first baby,' she reminded the mother-to-be. 'Nellie
can deliver all the rest as long as there doesn't appear to
be any problem.'

She smiled encouragingly but it had little effect.

'But we have a hospital now,' the woman argued.
'Andrew has made it really good, with a room for
operations and having babies.'

'You have a hospital but no nurse,' Christa reminded
her. 'Sister Jensen's at the hospital at Castleford. She's
delivered thousands of babies.'

'But Mick's so busy at the farm,' the woman pointed
out. 'And he wants to be with me for the baby—or afterwards, anyway.'

Christa smiled. Having babies was 'women's business'
to many of the people at Caltura, but even if Mick didn't
want to participate in the actual event it was understand-

able that the couple would want to be in the same place
for the birth of their first child.

'I'll talk to Jack about it,' she promised, although she
had no idea what he could do to solve the dilemma.
Andrew was right, she realised as she ushered the next
patient in. Caltura needed a nursing sister.

Her second pregnant patient was looking forward to
going to Rainbow Bay for her confinement. Her mother
lived there, she explained, and she enjoyed being spoilt
and fussed over for the last month of her term. Christa
looked at her file. This would be child number six! Was
the lure of her mother's attentions so great that she was
happy to keep producing babies?

Christa pronounced herself satisfied and saw the woman
out the door. Three small children claimed her with joyous
cries of 'Mum!' and, as she swung two of them into her
arms and the third attached itself to her skirt, Christa knew
that she'd been wrong. With such a brood, of course the
woman would enjoy a rest at her mother's place but her
love for her children was obvious.

A young girl sat outside the room, her hands twisting
at a handkerchief she held in her lap.

'You must be next,' Christa said, smiling at her and
waving her into the room.

The girl slipped through the door like a dark ghost,
betraying such agitation that Christa wondered if someone
had forbidden her to come.

'I know you, don't I?' she said, reaching for the patient
file. 'You're working as an aide at the school.'

The girl nodded.

Christa began to talk about the eye tests, repeating Ned's
opinion that the children's eyesight was very good. She
read quickly through the girl's file but, apart from visits
to the doctor for inoculations and once for a bout of fever

when she was a child, Carla Simpson had no medical history.

Slowly Christa worked around to what was troubling the girl, and was relieved when her problem of menorrhagia was hesitantly revealed.

'You're twenty,' she worked out from the file, surprised because Carla looked much younger. 'And how long has this been going on?'

'Two years now,' Carla admitted. 'Not all the time, but every few months too bad to go to work—to go anywhere.'

Christa considered the heavy blood loss Carla was experiencing, and wondered if she was also anaemic.

'I think you should come back to town when I go on Monday. I can radio from here and get someone to make an appointment with a specialist. There might be something wrong that a simple operation will cure.'

Carla began to twist her handkerchief again.

'I can't go on Monday,' she said, showing more determination than Christa would have expected in someone so shy.

'But the sooner you can be examined by a specialist the sooner we can fix whatever's wrong.'

'I could go in seven weeks—in the school holidays,' Carla said, her lips set in a stubborn line that told Christa there was no point in arguing. Carla had put up with the discomfort and inconvenience for two years so, to her, the seven weeks would be negligible. She gave in and wrote down the dates Carla could be in town.

'Well, I'll make arrangements for you to see someone then,' Christa told her. 'In the meantime, I could give you an oral contraceptive pill that should regulate things for you.'

Carla looked shocked at the thought of oral contraception, and Christa wondered about her background. Many of the young girls at Caltura were on the Pill, and contraceptive advice was readily available at the clinic.

'My family doesn't believe. . .' Carla quavered. 'My marriage is arranged in two years when my fiancé finishes at university. He will be a minister.'

'Taking an oral contraceptive for medical reasons isn't sinful,' Christa assured her, remembering that the ancestors of these local people had been converted by the missionaries at the original settlement and that a high proportion of the present generation held strong Christian beliefs. 'I have to take it myself to regulate my periods, and I'm not even engaged!'

She spoke lightly, hoping to ease Carla's concern, but speaking of it reminded her immediately of Andrew, and the anticipatory delight she'd managed to dispel during their peaceful morning's reverie by the lagoon returned in full force, coiling its way through her nervous system.

Carla eventually agreed to try Christa's suggestion, and went off with a month's supply and written instructions about when she was to begin the treatment.

Noises in the hall reminded Christa that it was breakfast-time. The fourth patient Jack had mentioned hadn't arrived so she tidied up, locked the room and crossed the hall to join Ned at a table set up at the far end near the kitchen. She was barely seated when Andrew arrived.

'I thought you were busy at the station,' she said, hoping that her words hid the silly grin twitching at her lips.

'I'll be busy later but this morning I want to watch Ned at work. I feel I should learn what to look for with trachoma in case we can't get a permanent nursing sister here.'

His matter-of-fact statement disturbed Christa, although she was at a loss to understand why.

'And are we under the tree again today?' Ned asked.

She shook her head.

'Jack suggested we use the hospital. It's time it was officially inaugurated and it has better lighting than the examination rooms we use here.'

Andrew took up the explanation. 'The main schoolroom has been converted into a ward with six beds—eight at a squeeze. The office stayed an office and the store-room remained a store-room, although it's big enough for two extra beds when there are visitors staying over. Out the back we've added a demountable building, brought in on the back of a semi-trailer. It has three rooms, one of which is an examination room—complete with a small X-ray machine—another is the "theatre" and the third is divided into shower and toilet cubicles.'

'I'm looking forward to working in my first "outback" hospital,' Ned told him, with a beaming smile. 'This whole experience is something else!'

Christa chuckled at his enthusiasm.

They finished their breakfast and walked across to the converted hospital. A group of people were assembled— some chatting in the shade at the bottom of the steps, while others sat on the verandah with their backs against the wall, dozing while they waited. Andrew stopped among them, talking quietly and unobtrusively checking the list Christa had given him on the plane.

Using her copy of the appointment list as a guide, Christa stacked the files they would need on a chair in the examination room. She switched on the bright lights above the table, and angled them so that they would provide maximum illumination without distracting glare.

Ned set up the equipment he required on a trolley, while she raided the store-room for sheets, swabs, kidney dishes and gloves. The shelves were well stocked with everything she could imagine the tiny 'hospital' would ever need, and most of the stores were not government equipment.

Again she wondered about Andrew. Had he found a 'money tree' that he could continue to provide such things for this community? He obviously had some source of wealth. And why was he doing it? Certainly not for the kudos other wealthy men might seek with loudly proclaimed 'donations' to worthy causes. No one outside the community and the RFDS knew of the changes he had achieved.

She ripped open the packaging on the new linen. What was even more perplexing was the elders' acceptance of his help. They'd turned away from government hand-outs, yet. . .

Maybe he's been 'adopted' —as she had—she decided, carrying the supplies back towards the examination room while she considered this solution.

The morning passed swiftly, and Ned proved an excellent teacher, showing Andrew and Christa the different kinds of evidence of trachoma in each patient they examined.

'See the grey areas in the cornea,' he pointed out. 'The disease was controlled before it caused permanent damage here. You can tell by the appearance of the conjunctiva and the fact that there was no significant contraction of tissues during healing.'

They passed on to a patient whose upper eyelid on his right eye had been affected by scar tissue. The eyelid had rolled inwards so that his lashes rubbed against the already damaged cornea, causing pain, surface lesions and scarring.

Christa noted him for surgery to repair the eyelid the following day, and as she looked up from the file she realised that Andrew had gone. She ignored the dart of disappointment. After all, he hadn't spent the morning in the hospital so that she could enjoy working with him nearby but so that he could learn something of use to the people.

By late afternoon, when the last patient had been seen, they had eight on the list for surgery. Christa, who had at least had an opportunity to sit down while she wrote file notes, felt the exhaustion in her legs, and wondered how Ned was faring.

'An early night for me tonight,' he told her when she enquired. 'I hope they're not intending to throw another party.'

'I shouldn't think so,' Christa told him. 'They've welcomed you and adopted me—that should be enough for one visit.'

They walked together back to the house, discussing their work in a desultory fashion.

'I'm going to sit on that chair and relax for half an hour,' Ned announced as they climbed the steps to the wide verandah. 'Just wake me in time to shower before dinner if I fall asleep.'

Christa agreed and moved on to her bedroom. She gathered up her towel and fresh underwear, and headed for the shower. Would Andrew be able to get down to see her tonight, or was he still too busy?

Or should she borrow a motorbike and go out to see him? She discarded the thought as she discarded her dirty clothes. If he had time to spare he would come to her. Wouldn't he?

Uncertainty began to eat away at the tentative happiness she'd been experiencing, adding to the doubts which so many unanswered questions had aroused. The whole situation was crazy, she decided as she washed away her weariness beneath the cool water. She went back to the beginning—to her first meeting with Andrew—trying to rationalise what was happening.

They'd worked together fortnightly for months, back when he'd declared himself responsible for seeing that people kept their medical appointments. She smiled at the enthusiasm which had swept all before it.

'We'll get a new bore,' he'd said, when she'd explained about trachoma spreading through lack of adequate washing facilities. A fortnight later he'd almost dragged her and Jack off the clinic plane.

Look,' he'd said, excited as a child as he'd shown them the clean artesian water pouring into a large tank.

'And over here!'

He'd led them to where two buildings had been patched up, and bright new plumbing installed.

'Until I can upgrade the plumbing and sanitation facilities in every house, we have. . .' he'd held up an imaginary trumpet in his hands and made a triumphant 'ta-ra' noise '. . .public bath-houses and toilets.'

Jack had congratulated him but Christa, even then, had sensed the force that propelled him along—wanting the best for the settlement, and wanting it yesterday!

'And what will you do when you've got the plumbing organised?' Jack had asked, half joking.

'I'll start on the cattle property,' Andrew had said, his commitment making the words into a pledge.

And she had seen less of him after that, although he had continued to chivvy the patients along to the community hall on clinic days and had usually returned to have dinner with the RFDS crew.

Again she smiled, lifting her head to feel the water wash across her face and remembering how they used to walk and talk after dinner. . .

Then last week he'd gone to Melbourne, come back to

Rainbow Bay, stayed at her place and lit unimaginable fires within her which continued to cause her major internal problems.

Had seeing his wife disturbed him in some way that he'd turned to the first available woman? Was his sudden talk of marriage between them a reaction to that meeting? A rebound reflex of some kind? And what had happened in his marriage—why was the wife he still seemed to care for shortly to become an ex-wife?

She turned off the shower, aware that no amount of thinking would provide her with the answers she sought. But when she was with him she forgot the questions, able to think only of the physical excitement with which his body was teasing, tempting and enticing hers.

He didn't appear at dinner time, so she and Ned ate in solitary splendour beneath the limp streamers and deflating balloons. Nancy and another two other women who had cooked and served their meal laughed and joked with each other, but the atmosphere at the table was less convivial as Ned picked tiredly at his food and Christa fought off the depression Andrew's absence had caused.

'We put on a dance night for you tomorrow,' Nancy announced, touching Ned on the shoulder as he prepared to leave the hall. 'Some of the young children who are learning will dance for you. Practice for Saturday night.'

With that cryptic statement she departed, and Ned turned to Christa.

'What's happening Saturday?' he asked.

'It's a house-opening,' she said, then shrugged. 'And don't ask me what that is because it's as much a mystery to me as it is to you.'

Ned thought for a moment, then turned back towards the kitchen.

'Excuse me, Nancy,' he called. 'What's a house-opening?'

She reappeared, wiping her hands on a small towel.

'House-openings happen when the spirit of a departed person finally goes, and the house can be used by someone else. Same as a name-opening when a dead person's name can be used again,' she explained, while the two helpers, who had emerged behind her, put their hands over their mouths and giggled—as if there might be more to things than this simple explanation.

'It's a big party. The men dig pits for a fire and we roast pig on hot coals in the ground. Lots of decorations and proper dancing to help the spirit leave,' Nancy continued.

She smiled at Ned.

'You should stay,' she suggested.

'I can't,' he said regretfully. 'I'm having my own version of a house-opening back at Rainbow Bay.' He turned to Christa. 'I'm shifting into a flat,' he added. 'All my gear has been in storage since I arrived, so I've been looking forward to sorting it out.'

'Never mind, you'll come again—maybe at some other party time,' Nancy assured him.

They said goodnight and walked away. Christa was wondering which house was being reopened—one of the shanties here near the airstrip, or one of the more modern, airy houses that were closer to the lagoon?

She was aware that Ned was talking, but her attention had strayed from houses back to Andrew and she missed the beginning of his conversation.

'. . .an attractive girl like you is already attached to someone?'

Heavens! Had be been asking her out?

She glanced at him, remembering that he was a visitor—

someone who was a long way from his home and new to the Bay. As she played the words over in her head she imagined that she could hear the loneliness in his voice.

But she couldn't help him! She was confused enough, trying to handle her own situation, without taking on a lonely Englishman as well!

'Well, I'm kind of attached!' she muttered, not knowing whether that was true or not! In any other circumstances Ned, with his quiet good looks, might have attracted her! 'But you'll soon meet plenty of women at the hospital. It's alive with single doctors and nurses, just waiting for a handsome Englishman to sweep them off their feet.'

'Maybe,' he said quietly, and she wondered if she'd been too flippant. She followed him up the steps to their temporary quarters, aware that the ease between them had been tilted askew by the halting conversation.

CHAPTER SEVEN

ANDREW was already at the lagoon when Christa reached it next morning, and this time he greeted her with a kiss.

Now was the time to ask about his wife, she thought, but as a bird cried its warning of their presence she knew that she couldn't break the spell the beauty of the place had bound around her.

'Let's sit,' he murmured, and she let him steady her as she sank to the ground then leant against him while the world took on the colours of daytime. Warmth passed between the places where their bodies touched, but it wasn't the heat of urgency they'd felt at the landing strip but more a contentment—a knowledge that soon there would be more than this.

'I love this place,' Christa whispered to him when the awakening was over and the sun began to heat her skin.

'I'm glad,' he whispered, and turned her so that their lips could meet.

'I'm glad,' he repeated more strongly, when the seductive bond of the kiss had been broken by a need to move on to the business of the day. Then once again he was gone, and she was left with more questions than she'd had before.

They began operating after breakfast, and Christa found herself remembering an assistant's moves from her training days in Theatre. Again Ned explained everything he did, detailing the complexity of the eye's functions as he worked.

'On some of the older men there's a hazing of the

cornea,' he said when they stopped for a tea-break between patients. 'I've never seen it before, but I'd guess it's keratopathy. It was common years ago in the far north of America, and was caused by reflected light off the snow.'

'These men wouldn't have seen snow,' Christa pointed out. 'Even in winter the daytime temperature rarely goes below twenty-eight degrees Celsius.'

Ned smiled, and shook his head.

'I'm beginning to realise how different things are here,' he agreed, 'but, in this case, I would assume that the reflected light off the barren ground would have the same effect.'

'So sunglasses should be more than a fashion accessory,' Christa suggested, and saw his emphatic nod.

'Everyone should wear them as protection, not only from the glare but from the harmful effects of the sun's rays. Our most recent research has shown that ultraviolet rays are as harmful to the eyes as they are to skin.'

She smiled at the passion in his voice and knew that he was a good doctor because his work obviously meant a great deal to him.

'We have volunteers who do "Sun-safe" talks to young children at our schools,' she told him. 'They emphasise wearing hats, protective clothing and sunscreen, and I believe they are now adding sunglasses to the list.'

They moved back to the small operating-room to greet their next patient, a comfortable familiarity growing between them as they worked together repairing the damage the trachoma had caused.

By three they were finished. Extra beds had been squeezed in so that all eight patients could stay overnight, and Ned sent Christa off to have a rest while he wrote up his notes on the files.

'On one condition,' she said when she agreed to take a

break. 'I'll stay here tonight, not you. It's nursing duties from here on in.'

He chuckled but acquiesced then turned back to speak to Nancy, who was helping in the ward—determined to learn as much medicine as she could before the doctor flew away.

Refreshed after her lazy afternoon, Christa waited for news of Andrew but there was no word and she was too uncertain of her role in his life to ask where he might be. After dinner she sat with Ned in the magical moonlight, watching the white-daubed children dance in the flickering firelight—entranced by the spectacle but again wishing she'd been able to share it with someone special.

Then it was Friday, and time for Ned to go. She walked with him to the airstrip where the small plane waited.

'Take the bandages off the uninjured eye if any patient becomes disorientated with both wrapped,' he reminded her. 'I've only bandaged both to stop muscle movement in the injured eye. By tomorrow the full bandages can come off. You can put clean dressings on the wound, and an eye-patch over the dressings. As long as the patients agree to come back for a fresh dressing on Monday you could release them after that.'

'And the three patients who had both eyes done?' she asked, wanting to check on the instructions one last time. 'Should I keep them in?'

'If they'll stay,' he replied, and she realised that he had come to know a great deal about these people in a short time. One of the older men was already fretting to be out of the strange environment, although his operation had been the most serious of the lot.

Christa said goodbye and watched Ned walk away.

If she'd met him a week earlier, would things have been different?

Another unanswerable question!

She waited until the plane lifted off the ground then turned back towards the hospital, where Nancy had appointed herself a nursing aide and was scolding the patients who dared to complain.

'I'll have my lunch and dinner here,' Christa told her. 'Whatever the women are fixing for the patients will do.'

'We're all organised, sister,' Nancy assured her and Christa smiled, wondering if it was her professional title or her new adoptive one that Nancy had used.

She went into the small office and wrote up Ned's instructions, aware that it was as important to keep records in a small place like this as it was in a city hospital.

Had Andrew organised the helpers for the hospital? she wondered as she watched Nancy bustle about, or had someone else taken over his role here when he had moved across to live at the out-station?

And so another day and night passed—the day easily because she was busy, but the night seemed endless as she tossed and turned on a folding bed in the store-room— within earshot of her patients.

All of whom were up, she realised as she walked through the 'ward' just after dawn. So there'd be no tryst by the water this morning, she thought, regretful yet somehow exhilarated by a new vibrancy in the atmosphere.

The patients' excitement hummed in the air, and she remembered that it was Saturday—the day of the big celebration. They spoke among themselves in dialect as they waited patiently for her to remove their bandages and examine the wounds and then, rebandaged, they left, eager to join in the preparations—all promising to return on Monday.

She stripped the beds and carried the linen through to the 'laundry'—a modern washing-machine incongruously set up on the back verandah. Once that was going she took the flammable rubbish down to the incinerator and burnt it, then sealed the used plastic and metal needles and syringes into a container to be taken back to town for secure disposal.

By lunchtime the hospital was clean and tidy, ready for its next influx of patients. But it couldn't have patients until it had staff, she remembered, and the thought caused a flicker of concern at the back of her mind, although she couldn't fathom why.

She ate the sandwiches Nancy had sent over for her and walked back to the schoolhouse, wondering about the evening ahead. She had packed two cotton dresses and had alternated them each evening for dinner. The rest of her wardrobe consisted of shorts, T-shirts and her uniforms. Nothing special for a celebratory event like a house-opening! She felt a pang of regret, and realised that she wanted to look her best for Andrew—if he came!

Sighing, she stripped off her uniform—crumpled from her night in the store-room—showered quickly and wrapped herself in a towel. Maybe she could sleep for a few hours.

Christa woke to a voice calling from outside, and roused herself. The towel had come undone and lay in a damp heap near her hips, but a sheet had been drawn over her. She tried to remember covering herself, then decided that it must have been an automatic action.

'You there?' a woman's voice called again and she secured the towel around her torso and crossed to the door, peering through the opening to see who was wanting her.

'I brought you feather-flowers, cousin,' her smiling visitor announced. 'For your hair, or round your neck.'

In her hands were a bunch of vividly coloured 'flowers', fashioned from the bright plumage of native birds.

'This one especially good in your hair,' the woman said, pulling a gleaming scarlet bud from the bunch. 'Black cockatoo.'

Christa remembered the birds flying above her as she'd watched day break over the lagoon. Beneath their tails had been brilliant wedges of red—the source of the feathers for her flower.

'Thank you so much,' she said. 'I'll be right out as soon as I've got some clothes on.' She motioned to the towel.

'It's OK, I'll leave them here,' her visitor replied, placing the colourful bouquet on the top step then scurrying away.

Christa felt disappointed. She would have liked to talk to the woman—maybe offered her a cup of tea from the small supplies provided for visitors. She pulled on shorts and a shirt, then went out on to the verandah. Off towards the lagoon she could hear the sound of voices, and laughter echoed back through the trees towards her. She knelt and touched the bright feathers, struggling against a feeling of loneliness that was threatening to overwhelm her.

Maybe she needed to be closer to her family. Had her new 'adoption' by Nancy reminded her of their closeness?

'So, you're awake!'

She looked up. Andrew stood at the bottom of the steps, a dusty figure in grubby shorts and shirt, his wide-brimmed stockman's hat set at a jaunty angle on his head and his feet apart, legs splayed.

'How did you know. . .?'

She hadn't finished the sentence before she realised how he knew and who had covered her. Heat flared, burning a path towards her cheeks. She glanced towards him and saw his teasing grin but his eyes were shadowed by his hat, hiding his innermost thoughts.

'I was tempted,' he admitted, tilting his head back and looking consideringly at her, 'just as I am now when I see you there—hair rumpled with sleep, your body still warm, your eyes so slumbrous.'

The words were like a physical touch and she thrilled to them, so easily tempted by his mastery at the game he was playing.

'Do you want to come in?' she said breathlessly, forgetting that there were things she wanted to ask—questions she felt needed answering.

'Not yet,' he said huskily, though he took a step closer and his hand reached out for the railing. 'Look at me—I'm filthy!'

Christa looked, but she didn't see the dust and dirt this time. She only saw the man who had tantalised her body beyond bearing. The sexuality which had woven its spell around her pulsed from him in unremitting waves, encircling her so tightly that she wanted to throw herself down the stairs and into his arms.

'Come in or go away!' she said, realising that she had reached the last vestiges of control. She knew that she should feel ashamed or embarrassed by her feelings yet, deep within, she sensed a rightness about this situation that she could not explain with words.

He stood and watched her for a moment, as if he could see her thought processes, then he smiled again and said, 'I'll be back at six to take you to the party.'

She watched him stride away and longed for evening. Did the 'why' of this strange attraction really matter?

Christa carried the flowers through to her bedroom, and looked at the plain navy dress she was going to wear. It had the understated elegance she liked in her more formal clothes—simple and unadorned. She frowned and shook her head. She'd look out of place at the party.

She glanced down at the flowers, then remembered the paper-stapler she'd used that morning in the office. She dashed across to the hospital and found it, then returned to her room and, ignoring possible damage to the fabric, stapled the flowers, one at a time, around the low, scooped neckline of the dress. The bright red bud she kept aside. She wasn't certain how she'd do it but—as her cousin had said—it would look good in her hair.

Would Andrew think she was mad? she wondered later, pulling on the decorated dress. She moved around in front of the mirror, trying vainly to get a fuller view of her appearance than the foot-square piece of glass could provide.

As far as she could tell, the flowers made her skin look paler but they definitely lent a festive air to her appearance. She smiled at herself and nodded, feeling the red bud move against her curls. She would be pleasing her adopted family and their friends—wasn't that as important as pleasing Andrew?

More important, part of her insisted. These people have given you a gift of friendship.

'Ready?' his clear voice called.

One last look in the mirror, all confidence gone.

'You didn't wait on the verandah when you visited this afternoon,' she said tartly, snapping off the bathroom light and walking down the shadowed hall towards him.

He held out a hand but she ignored it, feeling uncomfortable, overdressed and ridiculously ill at ease now that she was finally with him again.

'I did for a while,' he admitted, standing his ground, 'but when you didn't reply to my calls I walked in and checked each room.'

He paused and she thought she saw his chest move as

if he'd taken a deep breath. Then he smiled and added, 'And I closed my eyes before I stepped into the bedroom and pulled the sheet over you. Too much glorious temptation lying there for a man who had more work to do.'

There was another pause while he studied her, taking in every detail of her appearance and possibly gauging her mood as well.

'You look very partyish,' he said at last.

'And feel stupid,' she muttered, unable to believe that she could suddenly be overcome with such paralysing shyness after a week of lustful longings. 'Maybe I should take off the flowers.'

'The people who made them for you would be disappointed if you did,' he said quietly, but her uneasiness remained.

'And you, Andrew? Would you be disappointed, or do you think I'm being silly going to the party all decked out like this?' Her stomach twisted as she waited for his reply, yet it wasn't one of the important things she'd wanted to ask him. So why was she worried?

'Sit for a minute,' he said, and again he held out his hand.

This time she took it, and allowed him to steady her as she sat down on the top step. He seated himself beside her, rock-hard against one side of her body, but not holding her close.

'I had already answered that question,' he said slowly. 'I would be disappointed because I am one of the people.' He emphasised the personal pronouns and waited for a moment, as if giving her time to make a comment, then continued, 'I want you to be very aware of that, Christa, because it is important to me that I am seen that way.'

It answered some of her questions, she realised as she waited for him to finish what he wanted to say.

'I may look like any other dark-haired "white man", and I grew up thinking that's all I was. I lived thirty-two years without knowledge of my ancestors, then discovered some letters of my grandmother's—letters she had written to my mother when she married my father and moved to another town.'

Christa stirred beside him but he seemed unaware of her presence, staring out through the black silhouettes of the trees towards the noise and laughter echoing from the party site.

'My grandmother's mother had been a full-blood Aboriginal, a clever girl "chosen" by the missionaries on the station where she lived to be sent south and adopted by a white family. Can you imagine the effect it must have had on her—being taken from her family and from the beauty and serenity of the bush and thrust amongst strangers in a huge, cold city so far to the south?'

'I'd heard of it happening,' Christa murmured, trying to think of what she'd read about this practice. 'Weren't most of the girls trained to be servants? Wasn't the "adoption" a way of getting cheap household labour?'

He moved restlessly before he replied and, when he did, his voice was tight with emotion.

'She was luckier than many children who were treated this way, in that she was truly wanted and dearly loved. She grew up in privileged circumstances for the day, and photos I have since discovered show this ebony-dark child in the long white pinafores and pantaloons of the time, with white ribbons bobbing in her curly hair.'

He reached out and touched the red bud then his fingers lingered, running through Christa's curls and finally settling on the nape of her neck. It was a tentative touch—strange in a man who was always so assured—and she sat, immobile, not wanting to break whatever spell was prompting him to tell this story.

'She married a white businessman, a friend of her adopted family, but the social pressures of the time must have made things difficult. My grandmother's memories of her mother, according to her letters, are her strictures to stay out of the sun and a soft, hurting voice saying, "You don't want to be black like me!" It wasn't until she was very old that she talked to my grandmother about her homeland and her people, and told her tales she remembered hearing from her childhood.'

'And did your grandmother try to find out more? Or your mother? Did they know where she had come from? Her tribal history?'

Andrew shook his head.

'It's hard to trace that kind of thing because so few records were kept, although I doubt my mother or my grandmother tried. My grandmother died when I was too young to remember her, and my mother made no mention of an Aboriginal heritage during her life. It was only when she died four years ago that I found the letters among her personal possessions.'

Christa heard resentment and pain behind the words and she reached out and took his hand, kneading her fingers against his.

'She must have wanted you to know or she would have destroyed them,' she said.

'But why hadn't she told me earlier? Why let me grow up believing I was white?'

'You had that heritage as well—more of it,' she reminded him. 'And probably grew up in a middle-class environment where it was easier to be white. By keeping the knowledge from you until you were an adult, she was giving you a choice. It was then up to you to decide if you wanted to find out more or ignore that part of your blood-line. That's a decision a child couldn't make.'

His fingers moved against her neck and she heard him sigh.

What happened next? she wanted to ask, but she couldn't prise his story out of him. Whatever he offered must be freely given.

'We'd better go,' he said. 'They'll be wondering what's happened to us!'

Maybe I should have asked, she thought as he helped her up and held her hand as they walked towards the clamour of the celebrations.

'It took me a year,' he murmured, and she realised that he was talking about the decision. 'Then another two years of research in all my spare time to find out where my great-grandmother was born.'

'Caltura?' Christa asked, her footsteps slowing as she waited to hear the rest of the story before they were swamped by the revellers.

'Caltura!' he confirmed. 'Once I knew that the rest was easy. I came up to see the place, and understood both what the elders were trying to achieve and the impediments they faced—like lack of water and the money to make their project viable in the modern world.'

'It can only be viable if they become self-supporting,' Christa pointed out.

'Which can happen,' he argued. 'The cattle property has suffered because of bad management, but once it's back in full production it will provide work for the young people and an income for the settlement until their other projects—like the art school—are earning money.'

Christa smiled at the commitment in his voice.

'And you came back again to help it all happen.'

He stopped and turned towards her.

'It took me six months to organise my business affairs so they could be run by my managers in Melbourne, then I headed north. It was such a challenge, Christa! So exciting! If it had been an ordinary salvage operation—say a project to rescue the cattle station from bankruptcy—it would have been easy. It's working within the confines of what the elders want for the people, and what the people want for themselves, that makes it so special.'

'And so much hard work,' she added drily, seeing the lines of tiredness etched into his cheeks.

'I've never been afraid of hard work,' he said, and turned back to lead her into the circle of light around the huge camp-fire.

The emphasis on the final two words made her wonder what he did fear but when she looked at him, straight and tall—taking his place among his chosen people—she couldn't imagine him being afraid of anything.

The evening became a series of vivid impressions. Soft voices welcoming her; delicious food that made her feel lazily replete; the solidity of Andrew's body as she leant against him listening to the music—traditional this time, the low oompah of the didgeridoo throbbing its way through her blood.

The dancers mesmerised her, the firelight flickering on their painted bodies and feathered decorations so that the impression was of lighter-than-air spirit creatures weaving a story with their rhythmic movements. The trees around them were hung with balloons, and more feather flowers, streamers and woven ropes of native lilies—party decorations that took the best of both worlds.

And, beyond the firelight, above the decorated branches moon and stars spangled the world with their own special magic.

'It's nearly over,' Andrew whispered in her ear and she

stirred against him, shifting on the blanket he'd spread for
her to sit on, as the anticipatory delight she'd held at bay
throughout the evening began to swell within her.

'Is the house opened?' she asked, not knowing what
else to say.

'Well and truly,' he murmured, his lips against her hair.
'Would you like me to show you?'

She glanced around, realising that the crowd had thinned
considerably as people made their way to bed.

'Can we look?' she queried. 'Won't whoever it was
opened for be taking possession?'

She knew that it was a game; knew that they were both
putting off the moment when they would be alone together;
prolonging the delicious agony that was stretching between
them—pounding in their blood and dancing in their
nerves.

'I hope so,' he said, standing up and pulling her to
her feet.

He bent and picked up the blanket, shook the twigs and
leaves from it then folded it neatly over his arm.

More games, she thought as her tension hardened into
knots in her muscles.

'Come,' he said, and she allowed him to lead her into
the darkness beyond the fire's glow, then through a grove
of trees towards the dark outline of a small building.

CHAPTER EIGHT

IT WAS built up off the ground, as the hospital and school-house were, but only a few feet—enough to discourage snakes and be above water in the torrential rains of the Wet Season. They went inside and Christa smelled new-cut timber.

Then Andrew lit an old-fashioned hurricane lamp and she saw the room, large and airy, combining kitchen, dining-room and living-room in one. New pine cabinets and modern stove formed the kitchen, with a square pine table and four chairs marking the eating space. Near where they stood three easy chairs were grouped, inviting conversation—the whole giving the impression of a new, modern house awaiting occupation.

'That's it, apart from two bedrooms off this way with a two-way bathroom in between,' Andrew said. 'Shall we have a look?'

He led her across to a door that opened off the kitchen area and she gasped when she saw the wide double bed, spread with a snowy white crocheted cover. Beyond the bed were pine cupboards, and above it hung an Aboriginal painting that she knew must depict the lagoon.

Then Andrew turned her towards him and drew her into his arms, kissing her with a tenderness that made her toes curl. She put her arms around him and responded, feeling the fire flow through her veins as passion rose from the tenderness and began to engulf them both.

'Let's go to bed,' he managed to mutter against her lips some minutes later and she drew back, suddenly aware that they were in someone else's house.

He tugged at the zip that ran down the back of her dress, and she tried to stop him.

'Not here, we can't,' she whispered, although the feeling of his fingers on her skin, sliding—with the zip—down her spine, made the words weak and ineffectual.

'Here!' he whispered back. 'It's our house, Christa! The house of my great-grandmother's nephew, re-opened for us and furnished by me—for you.'

Doubt slammed inside her head. 'Our house'? But his fingers were sliding around her ribs, and her breasts ached for his touch. You're going too fast, she wanted to say, but thought that he might misunderstand and stop the tantalising physical assault—which was going too slowly!

He stripped off her clothes, then stood and waited until she understood that he wanted her to do the same for him. With fumbling fingers she undid buttons, but once his shirt was removed her panic increased.

'I can't do this. I'm no good at it,' she mumbled, then his hands closed over hers, guiding her to take his zip and slide it down as slowly as he had lowered hers. She shook with tension as she felt him draw her closer, choreographing her movements as she slid her hands against his silky skin, easing his trousers down—catching at the elastic of his undershorts to take them at the same time.

She'd stopped breathing, she knew that much.

The lantern flickered in the other room, providing only the faintest of illumination in the bedroom, but it was enough to see the muscle shapes beneath his skin; enough to know that his excitement was as great as hers, his need for her as strong as hers for him.

He led her to the bed, pulling back the covers and pushing her down onto the sheet—holding her there while he studied her for a moment. Her hands scrabbled for the cover as other memories intruded. Memories of discomfort, pain—and disappointment.

'I'm no good at this,' she cried again when his fingers closed over hers, denying her the protection she'd sought. 'He said—'

'Hush,' he said, and covered her lips with his hand, his little finger finding its way to the tender skin inside her lower lip and sliding along the silky moistness.

His free hand brushed across her skin, feather-soft, teasing at nerve endings until the tiny hairs stood up along her arms and her blood thrummed feverishly in her veins.

Embarrassed by his scrutiny, even in this dim light, she reached up and pulled him down on top of her, and the time for slow exploratory moves was over.

Now they kissed, their bodies pressed together, moving on each other as skin explored skin, tongue explored tongue and hands roved in their own journeys of discovery, sliding and seeking—finding the secret parts of the body that aroused and intensified pleasure.

They spoke occasionally—murmurs of delight or reassurance, questions and answers, lips moving on lips.

'Please, Andrew,' Christa murmured at last when the pleasure-pain had become unendurable.

She eased her legs apart to take him and felt his heat explode inside her. He pressed his hands beneath her, lifting her to the rhythm of his movements. She found the pace and moved herself, feeling a tension building and building—a strange plateauing tightness of nebulous delight that she wanted to cling to for ever.

Then the movements changed and he thrust deep inside her, again and again, until the world exploded and shivers of release sped like quicksilver through her body to tingle in every nerve ending. She heard her voice cry out, a combined lament of greatest exaltation and deepest loss, and she shuddered in his arms as he groaned and fell against her in the aftermath of his own release.

They lay entwined in silence, while Christa wondered what had happened and tried to piece herself together after the shattering experience.

Then Andrew kissed her, a silent pledge, and moved to lie beside her, turning her so that she was nestled up against him—curled into his body with his warmth flowing into her.

'That's never happened to me before,' she whispered into the darkness, so moved by the experience that she had to say something!

His arms tightened in response, but when he said, 'Have you tried all that often?' in a harsh, unforgiving kind of voice she knew that it had been a mistake—and one she had to try to remedy.

'Only with Daniel,' she whispered, pulling away from him—wanting him to hold her for ever, yet not wanting his securing clasp if he thought that she was the kind of woman who drifted from bed to bed.

He released his hold on her, and left the bed. Christa shivered, upset that she had broken the spell of wonderment between them yet angry that the truth could do this so easily.

He was back within minutes with the lamp, held at shoulder height, casting a shaft of golden light across the bed.

He set it on a high shelf above the bed, and dimmed it so that the shadows darkened the outer edges of the room but their faces were discernible.

He drew the sheet up over her, tucking it around her shoulders as if she were a child, then knelt so that he could look into her face.

'I'm sorry, Christa. Sorry I hurt you then. I had no right

to say that,' he said quietly. 'Your future is my business, not your past.'

His fingers pushed the hair back from her forehead, and he traced her eyebrows and drew his thumbs across her cheek-bones.

His eyes were shadowed by the lamp behind and above him so that she could not see their colour. The mention of the future caused a fluttering in her heart, but the pads of his thumbs were now moving on her lips and she could only tremble under the touch.

'But you were right not to marry Daniel,' he added gruffly. 'No man should make a woman feel that way—unloved, frustrated, even inadequate—especially not woman as vibrant, and loving and generous as you.'

'He wasn't one for thinking of others,' she admitted, talking against—and licking at—the palm of the hand that lingered near her mouth. 'As far as he was concerned I was a belonging—like the car he'd been given for his eighteenth birthday, or the boat he'd received for his twenty-first. He was under no obligation to give them pleasure.'

'Oh, Christa!' Andrew murmured, and reached up to turn the lamp out, before sliding into bed beside her and drawing her into the warm comfort of his arms. 'Let me make it up to you,' he whispered. 'Let me help you learn the ways our bodies can please each other. The taking and giving of physical pleasure is one of the greatest of gifts marriage can provide, along with companionship and common goals.'

Was he so certain of that from his own experience? The thought stabbed through her and she knew that there were more questions she wanted to ask, more answers she needed to hear. But his hands drifted across her shoulders, her arms and the base of her spine, lulling her out of her anxiety—confusing her mind with hints of the pleasures he spoke about, with promises of still greater delights to come.

'You speak as if the future is already settled,' she murmured sleepily, turning so that she was again snuggled up against him.

'Isn't it?' he responded, his fingers dancing erotically across her breasts. Tired as she was, she felt the tug his teasing caused. 'Wasn't this test enough that we'd be compatible?' His voice grew deeper and his hands slid lower to linger on her thighs and gently brush across the mound between them. 'Or should we try again to make doubly certain?'

'Too tired,' she muttered as sleep caught at her mind and jumbled her thoughts and uncertainties.

His lips pressed against her neck, as if accepting her decision and bidding her goodnight, and she felt her love for him glow through her body.

They slept and woke to love again, moving with each other more easily this time—taking special pleasure now that some of the urgency had abated.

At ease once more, they lay together—watching dawn lighten the sky beyond the wide window.

'Have you patients to see or would you like to come over to the out-station and see what we've been doing there?' he asked, his fingers trailing up and down her arm and setting fire to the skin beneath the gossamer touch.

'I'd like that. I've no patients until tomorrow,' she told him, her body skittering with excitement as she thought of riding behind him again—pressed against his body thigh to thigh—on the dusty bike he used as transport.

'I'd better go back to the schoolhouse and find some more suitable clothes,' she added, although she didn't want to move from the security of his arms.

'Do you want to go now—before people are up and about?' he asked, and she turned and propped herself on one elbow so that she could look down into his face.

With the tip of one finger she traced his profile—forehead, nose and chin—then brought the finger back and moved it around the outline of his lips.

'You're asking if I'm embarrassed or ashamed in some way, aren't you?' she said slowly, searching through her thoughts while she tested the question.

His eyes were watchful, fixed on her face, ready to read the slightest hint of untruth.

She smiled at him and knew that the love she felt was probably shining in her eyes, but this was no time for hiding things.

'I'm probably a bit embarrassed,' she admitted, 'but I'll pull on my party dress and walk back to the schoolhouse without any shame.'

She leant forward and pressed a kiss on his lips, then moved back again to study his face in turn.

'What's happened between us is many things, Andrew,' she said quietly, wanting truth between them. 'It's unexpected and, for me, has been very special, but I can't see it as shameful—can you?'

He muttered something unintelligible and pulled her down on top of him, kissing her so thoroughly that the need sprang up again and it was a long time before she pulled on her dress and walked back to the schoolhouse to shower and change into shorts for the ride to the outstation.

She was combing the tangles out of her wet hair when a commotion outside told her she had visitors.

A tall man she did not recognise was standing at the bottom of the steps with a crying child in his arms.

'He's got a belly-ache,' the woman with him told her. 'Bad!'

Christa hurried down, and reached out to feel the child's forehead. It was burning hot.

'Bring him over to the hospital,' she said, and led the way, waving the man into the examination room and gesturing for him to put the child on the table.

The young boy lay there limply for a moment, then cried out and pulled his knees up against his chest. The man groaned and raced away, obviously too distressed to stay and watch the suffering of his son.

Christa ran her hands across the slight body, feeling the tightness of his stomach and seeing his flinching reaction when she pressed on his lower abdomen.

The tenderness and temperature added up to appendicitis. She sent the boy's mother to the store-cupboard for clean hand-towels, and was grateful when Andrew appeared to offer his support.

'Wet them under the tap, wring them out, then hold them against his forehead and wipe them over his body,' she told the woman. 'We need to bring his temperature down.'

The woman nodded and disappeared.

'What can I do?' Andrew asked, his deep voice sending tremors of delight through every cell in her body.

'Could you watch him while I get on to the Base? Talk to him and keep him calm,' she replied. She was thankful for his unobtrusive support, and calmed by his presence.

Hurrying to the hospital transceiver, she hit the emergency call button and repeated the Caltura call sign. Caltura was one of the blind spots in the cellular network, and one of the few places still reliant on radio.

Surprisingly enough a voice responded immediately, an unusual occurrence at nine on a Sunday morning, but

Christa didn't waste time asking Katie what she was doing at work.

'It's an inflamed appendix, possibly ruptured,' she told Katie. 'He needs urgent attention.'

'I'll page a pilot, then get through to Jack,' Katie's placid voice assured her. 'He's gone north to pick up a couple injured when their car rolled over on Herd Island. I'll call you back in a few minutes.'

Christa delegated one of the family to sit by the radio, and returned to her patient.

'I'm going to give you something to make you feel better,' she told the child, noticing how trustingly he looked at her now that Andrew was there to hold his hand. She turned away from the unexpected poignancy of the sight to unlock the cabinet where the supplies she'd brought from town were stored.

Her mind was racing as she pulled out a bag of fluid, painkillers and antibiotics. She ripped the seal from a disposable thermometer, and walked back to take the boy's temperature. It was 41°C and she felt panic jolt through her as she recalled lessons learnt long ago. A slight rise in temperature was a symptom of appendicitis—a major rise was evidence of peritonitis. Start antibiotics and electrolytes, her training told her, and at that moment someone called her to the radio.

'Eddie's on his way,' Katie told her. 'Jack said to start fluid and antibiotics immediately, but nil by mouth. Susan is with Jack on the big plane and Jane's away, so he wondered if you can come back with the boy.'

A request I can't refuse, Christa realised. She could hardly send a sick child and a probably panicky mother back on the plane without support.

'That's OK,' she answered, although—for the first time she could recall—she felt resentful of her work and regretful that it was going to steal her precious day with Andrew.

She signed off and hurried in to her patient, swabbing his arm and inserting a fluid line. She lifted a drip stand into place at the side of the couch and started the fluid, adding the antibiotics so that they could drip into his veins at a steady rate. Andrew moved aside when necessary but remained where he could touch the boy; and all the time he chatted softly, using the local dialect as naturally as if he'd grown up speaking it.

Christa explained what was happening to his parents and waited until the mother hurried away to pack a bag for herself and the boy, before turning to another onlooker and asking them to find Nancy and bring her up to the hospital.

'I'll have to go back to town with him,' she explained to Andrew. 'If Nancy can handle the new dressings for the post-op patients I wouldn't have to fly back.'

'Don't want to come back, huh?' he teased, and the gleam in his eyes looked like love.

Her stomach scrunched into a tight ball and her mouth grew dry with desire.

'I've other things to do,' she whispered huskily, 'like work!'

He smiled at her and nodded, and she knew that he also had work to do. In all likelihood she wouldn't have seen him tomorrow anyway!

'Go get your bag,' he said. 'I'll watch the drip.'

She dashed away, escaping the weakness of the hunger he could arouse so easily. Back at the house, she threw her clothes into her overnight bag and cast a quick glance around the house to make sure that she had left it tidy.

She carried her bag over to the hospital. The boy's mother had returned and taken Andrew's place by his side. Christa checked her patient quickly, then walked through to the office to sort out the drugs Nancy might need.

'You want me?'

She looked up from this task and saw her new 'sister', hovering uncertainly in the doorway.

'Yes, Nancy,' she said, straightening up and stacking the drugs on the desk. 'I have to go to town with the child. You helped me with the dressings yesterday. Do you think you can do them on your own when the patients come back tomorrow?'

'I'll stay here and help her,' a deep voice said, and Christa spun around to see that Andrew had reappeared.

His grey eyes looked smoky—as they did when he was aroused—and his lips twitched with a wry amusement, making the bones in her knees turn to water.

She smiled at him and shrugged, trying to hide the disappointment that threatened to overwhelm her.

'Thanks,' she managed to mutter.

He moved his head in an almost imperceptible gesture, and she said to Nancy, 'Would you go back and keep an eye on the boy while I set up all the equipment you'll need on a trolley?'

She left the office and followed Andrew into the store-room. He kicked the door closed and drew her into his arms, embracing her with a desperation that had little to do with desire.

'What a bloody awful courtship!' he mumbled, moving his chin against her hair while his hands wandered fever-ishly over her body, as if seeking to imprint their knowledge of it in his mind.

'I can't get away again until after the cattle sales next month and you won't be back until the next clinic flight, and even then you'll be working all day and only here for one night!'

'We'll manage,' she said shakily, overwhelmed that it

seemed as if he was going to miss her as much as she knew she would miss him.

'Will we?' he growled, and drew back so he could tilt her head up to his demanding kisses.

'We'll have to,' she stammered when she finally caught enough breath to form words.

'This time!' he said, the words a deep promise of some kind. 'This time!'

CHAPTER NINE

CHRISTA pulled reluctantly away, and heard Andrew open the door. Hurriedly she assembled what Nancy would need for the dressings, setting the packaged swabs and bandages in order.

'Make sure she burns the soiled dressings and the swabs she uses.' She hoped that he couldn't hear the disappointment in her voice and turned to look at him, standing with his arms folded in the doorway—looking outward, not inward.

'I'll make sure,' he said, all businesslike again—which made her feel ashamed of her own remnants of excitement and her jolting impatience that work had to come first.

She spread a clean sheet across the loaded trolley and pushed it against the shelves.

'The plane will be here soon,' she said to Andrew, and knew that she wanted to spend a last few precious moments in his arms.

Could she make that first move? Kick the door shut as he had done earlier? He spoke of a 'future' for them, but she barely knew him! Certainly she didn't know him well enough to guess how he'd react if she took that initiative! The thought saddened her and she fidgeted unnecessarily, straightening already tidy piles of equipment on the shelves.

'I'll go out to the landing ground and make sure the strip's cleared,' he said at last, then he turned and kissed her lightly on the cheek before striding away.

Fighting off her own dissatisfaction, Christa returned to her patient.

'Can you carry him across to the plane?' she called to the father who had returned, and was hovering by the door. She saw his answering nod. 'I'll tell you when,' she told him, and crossed to the sink to wet more towels for the journey back to Rainbow Bay.

Packing them into a plastic bag, she wondered if she and Andrew stood a chance of forming a proper relationship. GI, she remembered from her teenage years— geographically impossible. Back then it had alluded to meeting a boy who lived on the other side of a city, where public transport was irregular at best and non-existent after sunset and the distance too far to cover by push-bike— their pre-car-licence form of transport.

She heard the drone of an engine, and nodded to the man. One of the relatives picked up her overnight bag, and another took the equipment case. She unhooked the fluid bag and held it above the boy as they made their way, like a straggling procession, towards the airstrip.

She saw Andrew walk hurriedly to the plane as it stopped. He had the door open before Eddie left the cockpit.

'Quick visit,' Eddie said to him as Christa led the others into the plane, and indicated to the father to put the boy on the stretcher.

He lowered his son with such anxious tenderness that she found her eyes smarting as she watched the big, work-roughened hands linger on the child's body.

She hooked up the fluid bag, strapped the cases into place, led the quiet mother to a seat and then watched as those who would remain behind moved quickly down the steps.

Eddie and Andrew were walking around the plane, talking, while Eddie did a visual check.

I can hardly run back down the steps and kiss him goodbye, Christa thought. Or could I?

She remembered what she'd said about shame and embarrassment and was tempted, but then the child cried out so she turned her attention to him, removing the warm, drying towels and packing cool wet ones around him.

Eddie came on board, pulling the door up behind him and locking it.

'All set?' he said to Christa and, with a last, longing look out of the window, she echoed his words.

'All set!' she said, while her heart denied it. She'd never been less 'set' in her life.

She strapped herself into her seat and pulled out a file, filling it in while the plane accelerated—taking her away from the place where she wanted to be and the person with whom she wanted to remain.

And that thought brought its own demons to torment her. Could she commit her future so impetuously to a man she barely knew? Was it solely sexual attraction that was drawing her into the net Andrew seemed to have cast about her? She was old enough, surely, to know the difference between love and attraction—but was she experienced enough?

'OK!' Eddie called, signalling that seat belts could be unstrapped if she wanted to tend her patient.

She put aside the tormenting questions and concentrated on work. She would have plenty of time to think about personal matters over the next week. Right now, she was on duty once again!

An ambulance was waiting when they arrived back at the Bay and Christa, sensing that the mother was feeling wary and insecure in the strange environment, accompanied the pair to the hospital.

'They'll take him straight to Theatre,' she explained to the woman as they drew up at the emergency entrance. 'I'll fill in all the forms for his admittance, then wait with you.'

The woman smiled for the first time since Christa had met her, and reached out to grasp her hand.

Feeling the thin fingers grip hers, Christa thought of kinship—of sister, cousin, uncle, aunt! The warmth she'd felt when Nancy had 'adopted' her sprang back to life, and she returned a gentle, reassuring pressure.

'Takes longer than the operation—all this paperwork,' the admitting clerk said sympathetically. 'When he comes out of Recovery they'll take him to the children's ward. There's a waiting-room and some food and drink dispensers up there.'

They went up to the children's ward and Christa led the woman, Dawn, to the waiting-room and fixed her a cup of strong, sweet tea.

'Are you hungry?' she asked, eyeing the assortment of snacks that could be had for a dollar coin and the manipulation of dials and buttons.

'No,' Dawn murmured, her dark eyes darting nervously about the room as if unknown terrors might lurk in the colourfully painted corridors or behind the bright curtains.

'Did you have your babies here?' Christa asked.

Dawn shook her head.

'Castleford,' she explained. 'Three babies, all there.'

Christa smiled. Castleford had a six-bed hospital with one nursing sister and two aides. No wonder Dawn was intimidated by her surroundings. She sipped at her own tea, and thought about the newly imposed isolationist policy at Caltura. Should it be leavened with some visits to town?

'Sam's been here more than me,' Dawn said, nodding

her head towards the children's ward as she spoke of
her son.

'In hospital?'

'No! School of Distance Education camps,' Dawn
explained. 'All the kids come to town once a year for a
week. The teachers come with them!'

'I'd heard about that,' Christa replied, remembering also
that many of the older children came to town for secondary
and tertiary education.

They chatted on as Dawn's shyness in her new surroundings gradually eased. By the time Sam came back to the
ward Christa was satisfied that the woman would be
all right.

'Have you friends or relatives in town?' she asked when
the ward sister shooed them away so that Sam could sleep.

'I'll stay here,' Dawn told her as they walked back
towards the waiting-room. 'Sister said I can sleep in the
chair near his bed, and there's plenty of food in the
machines and a bathroom down the hall. I'll be OK.'

'You could stay at my place,' Christa offered, but she
wasn't surprised when Dawn refused. She wanted to be
where she could reach out and touch her child, and Christa
could understand her feelings.

'Then I'll call in and see you tomorrow,' she promised.
She crossed to retrieve her overnight bag from under a
chair. Unzipping a side pocket, she felt with her fingers
for a pen and small notebook which she kept in that com-
partment. Extracting them both, she jotted down her phone
number and gave it to Dawn.

'Phone me if you are worried about anything,' she said.
'I'm off duty for the next three days, so I'll be at home
most of the time.' The three days seemed endless, and an
unfamiliar loneliness assailed her.

She walked away with a curious reluctance, as if, in

leaving Dawn and Sam, she was severing the last link between herself and Andrew.

'Don't be silly,' she told herself while she waited for the lift that would take her back to the ground floor.

The days off dragged by. She cleaned her house from top to bottom, and spent hours at the hospital with Dawn. Her mind had figured that if she kept her body busy it would be tired enough to sleep through the night, but the theory proved false and she would twist and turn in her bed at night—memories of Andrew's touch inflaming her senses until sleep was impossible.

And the hours of darkness brought no solace from her own disruptive thoughts. How had this happened so suddenly? Had the rash of engagements and weddings among people she knew mellowed her enough for Andrew's onslaught on her senses to be so readily accepted?

And what had happened to his first marriage? She remembered the words he'd used about marriage—about the giving and receiving of pleasure. So, what had gone wrong that he'd left a son he obviously adored and moved to such a remote location? Had he been escaping his own misery—running from too many memories? Was it pain and anguish—caused by lost love—that had caused him to seek out his great-grandmother's people?

Christa would shake her head when her thoughts took her this far, and smile. She might not know him well, but she knew that he wasn't a man who would run from his problems. He was a fighter, not a quitter.

'Caltura, Monday,' Jack reminded her when they met at the Base on Wednesday afternoon. 'Anything special we need to take?'

She shook her head.

'I'm officially off duty,' she reminded him, 'but I came

in to check the files—three babies due for triple antigen, and you might like to have a look at Carla Simpson.' She explained the treatment she had offered Carla and Jack listened, then agreed that the young woman needed to see a specialist.

'I'll take a blood sample too,' he said. 'You're right, she could be anaemic. I can check that on site and make a note for the specialist to do a full blood count when she comes to town.'

'So I'll put her on the list? And what about the eight people who had the eye operations—will you see them?'

Jack agreed with both suggestions, then frowned at her.

'What are you doing here if you're off duty?' he asked, as if her first words to him had suddenly assumed a meaning.

'I wanted to do the appointment lists to go out on tomorrow's mail plane,' she explained, and prayed that she wasn't doing anything as adolescent as blushing at the same time.

'You could have phoned Leonie,' he pointed out. 'She's done the lists before.'

Christa shrugged.

'It was easier to work it out with the files,' she said, but she knew that she'd come because she was debating whether she'd tuck a letter to Andrew in with the lists. Would he see them or was he so busy at the out-station that Nancy or his deputy would handle the appointments? Would he know her handwriting if he did see them, and guess that she'd been thinking of him?

Stupid female! she chided herself. She usually typed the lists! And, if she wanted to send a message, she could write to him—couldn't she?

Yet writing to him seemed such a 'forward' thing to do! She sighed. It all came back to her own uncertainty.

So she sat in the office, surrounded by Caltura files, and thought about Caltura. If they'd had a nurse at the hospital Sammy and Dawn could have gone home on the mail plane, but as it was they'd have to wait until Monday and go back on the clinic flight.

The thought of Monday made her pulse leap, then she remembered that tomorrow's mail plane brought mail back from Caltura as well. Maybe he would write.

She was back on duty Thursday, on call from six the previous evening, and called out at midnight.

'It's a local job,' the answering service told her. 'Young man with a suspected broken neck they want transferred from the Bay to Brisbane for specialist treatment and rehabilitation. Ambulance will be at the airport in thirty minutes.'

It was an easy job in that her patient was already stabilised. Her part in the procedure was to keep him as comfortable as she could during the three-hour flight, and reassure him about the future if he woke from his medication-induced sleep. It proved an uneventful trip, she and Michael sharing a pizza at four in the morning at Brisbane airport before they turned around and flew back to the Bay.

She slept on the plane and was grateful that she had as they touched down in Cairns, changed pilots and were off again—this time north to Wyrangi for another transfer, a tourist with shotgun pellets in his chest and shoulder.

'That sounds like something different,' Eddie remarked when she settled into the copilot's seat for the flight.

'I didn't get any further explanation,' Christa told him. 'I just hope it was a self-inflicted accident, or the result of fooling around with his mates.'

'Rather than an irate property owner up there, taking the law into his own hands?'

'Precisely!' Christa turned to watch Eddie as he eased the plane up, up, up into the air. 'With the influx of tourists into the area, the more adventurous travellers are looking for new places to explore and you can't blame the locals for trying to protect their boundaries.'

'With shotguns?' Eddie smiled at her and shook his head.

Christa returned the smile. 'I think fences might be better, or a sign saying "Private Property".'

They were met at Wyrangi airport by the hospital sister, Joan Campbell, in the big State Emergency Service truck that doubled as an ambulance.

'I've given him a painkiller, but nothing else,' Joan explained. 'I used local anaesthetic to get the pellets out of the soft tissue in his upper arm and shoulder, but where they've struck bone, or are more deeply imbedded, I thought I'd better leave them until he gets to a surgeon. Jack could have done the job here if it had happened during one of his visits.'

Christa watched as three helpers loaded the overweight young man on to the plane.

'How did it happen?'

Joan shrugged.

'Maybe you'll have better luck finding out than I did,' she replied. 'His story is that he was fooling around and the gun went off, catching him in the shoulder, but—even without forensic training—I think the damage would have been much greater if that had happened.'

'So, what's your guess?' Christa prompted.

'Well, he was travelling with a group—two other young men and two girls. I'd say there was an argument. He was far from sober when he was brought in, and his "mates" dropped him off with his gear and disappeared.'

'You can't disappear from Wyrangi,' Christa pointed

out. 'It's a five-hour drive to the nearest settlement, and there's only one road. Your policeman could have picked them up on the road, or had someone hold them at the next town.'

'If it had been murder he probably would have,' Joan agreed. 'But a fairly minor injury? I suppose if he'd accused one of the others of taking a pot-shot at him it would have been different.'

'Ready to go,' Eddie called, and Christa said goodbye to Joan and climbed back into the plane, shutting and locking the door behind her.

'How often do planes fly out of Rainbow Bay?' the young man asked as she reached over him to check the stretcher locks. His eyes were hooded, hiding all expression, but there was something in his voice that made her shiver.

'Depends where you want to go,' she told him lightly, picking up his file and settling into a seat across the aisle from him. 'Four flights a day south, and a couple west to Mt Isa. Now, I'm Christa, and you're—' she checked his file '—John Gordon?'

He looked blankly at her for a moment then nodded, and she wondered if he'd made up the name or if his 'friends' had given it to him when they'd dropped him at the hospital. His eyes were blue, she'd noticed in that instant, and as cold and lifeless as marbles.

'Are there flights to Ruthven?' he asked, naming the town south of Wyrangi towards which his friends would be heading.

'The mail plane goes there once a week,' she told him, 'or you can charter a plane. Do you want to meet up with your friends?'

'Yes,' he said and closed his eyes, effectively ending any conversation between them.

She was concerned as she supervised his transfer to the ambulance at the Bay, but couldn't pin down an instinctive feeling that something was wrong.

'He's not your problem any longer,' the ambulance man said cheerfully, as if he sensed her disquiet. 'The boys at the hospital will take care of him.'

She did her 'housekeeping' on the plane, then went across to the small office in the hangar and filled out requisition forms to replace drugs and dressings she'd used on the two flights. She was frowning out across the tarmac when Eddie joined her in the room.

'Not like you to be sitting about brooding,' he joked.

'No?' she said, turning to him with a half-smile. 'Sometimes it seems that's all I do these days.'

'You worried about that chap?' he asked.

Christa thought for a moment before answering.

'That's definitely part of it,' she said, then realised that it was one part she could do something about. 'I think I'll drive over to the hospital, visit young Sam and maybe have a word with someone over there.'

She left the forms for Eddie to drop off at the Base, and drove over to the hospital. Then she realised that she had no idea who to see about her inexplicable and probably quite groundless fears.

'Is the patient welfare officer available?' she asked, when faced with the decision at the reception counter.

A quick phone call proved that she was. Christa was directed to an office on the ground floor, and knocked on a door that gave the officer's name as Gail Webster.

'So what do you think we should we do?' Gail asked, when Christa had stumbled through her explanation.

'I've no idea,' she admitted, 'but I felt I had to talk to someone. Could you find out if he's using his real name? Do you need to ask for proof of identity for any reason?

Do you usually contact a patient's family? Would that be normal procedure?'

She felt stupid, sitting in the office of this obviously busy woman and trying to convey the feelings that those cold blue eyes had generated.

'We contact the family if the patient is unable to do it for him- or herself. But why are you worrying? Are you saying he might have a police record?' Gail asked.

'I don't know what I'm saying,' Christa replied, 'but he frightened me, and I thought I should at least pass on that thought.'

'Well, we'll see what we can do,' Gail said, her tone of voice indicating an end to the conversation.

Christa left the room feeling dissatisfied, but what else could she do? She took the lift up to the children's ward and visited Sammy, sitting for a while and letting Dawn's chatter about the nurses and other patients soothe her mind.

'He's well enough to be at home,' she said as she watched Sam playing with the other children.

Dawn nodded.

'They'll let him out tomorrow. We might go to friends of my husband. They live in town, but I haven't met them.'

'Come to my place,' Christa urged, knowing that their company would help her through the endless hours of the weekend. She reached into her pocket and found a pen, then picked up a paper napkin off Sam's lunch tray.

'Here's the address. I'll leave the key with my next-door neighbour at number sixteen, and you can get a cab over whenever you like. My dog, Wally, lives there half the time, so he'll probably greet you and will keep Sam occupied.'

Dawn smiled shyly at her.

'Are you sure?' she asked.

'Certain!' Christa told her, then wondered if Dawn had

enough money for a taxi—and how she was going to raise such a delicate subject!

'Mum, can I get a drink from the machine?' Sam asked, coming across to them with another boy who had his money clutched in his fist.

'I've got change,' Christa said quickly. 'I don't suppose you had time to think about money before you left Caltura.'

Dawn smiled at her.

'I have plenty of money,' she assured Christa. 'I did bring some with me, but Andrew came yesterday and he gave me more. He set up a bank account for people to draw on who have to come to town.'

Andrew came to town yesterday? The words hammered in Christa's head. Maybe he'd called her and she'd been out!

Of course she hadn't been—except for the short time when she'd driven to the Base to go through the Caltura files and do the lists.

'. . .Andrew fixed it with the hospital some time ago so Caltura patients, especially in an emergency, don't get stuck here with no money.'

Dawn chattered on, while the words swirled through Christa's head.

She worked at the Base—he'd have known where to contact her if she wasn't at home!

'. . .so wonderful, so thoughtful. Thinks of things that might embarrass us. . .'

Wonderful and thoughtful—but not wonderful enough to call and say hello—or don't I count? Can he so compartmentalise his life that I couldn't be included in this visit?

The realisation that she knew so little of this man she'd virtually flung herself at slammed into her like a thunderbolt.

'. . .back from Melbourne. His wife lives there, you know.'

Christa tried to drag her mind back into focus. Did everyone else know more about his wife than she did? And how did they know? Did he talk more to others than he did to her?

Those things were bad enough, but the final question hurt the most. Knowing of his wife, what would the people she liked and respected at Caltura think of her behaviour?

Devastation, so extreme that it made her bones ache, flooded through her. She could hear his voice lamenting the shortness of time they had together—explaining that he couldn't leave Caltura until after the cattle sales. Yet he'd been to Melbourne!

'I've got to go. Appointment!' she mumbled at Dawn, and hurried away before shock gave way to tears—or worse, to rage!

He'd never said anything about love, she realised as she sat in her car, trying to gather enough composure to drive home with relative safety. But he had spoken of marriage, and he had made love to her with a passion that had left him spent and trembling in her arms.

And she'd been foolish enough to think that it added up to love!

'Of course,' she said aloud, 'he might have been called to Melbourne suddenly.'

But even saying it aloud didn't make it sound believable.

She took a deep breath and started the car, blocking out the agony of uncertainty with thoughts of her strange, cold-eyed patient and the explanation of the shotgun wound that didn't ring true.

Instead of going home she drove to the Base. Jack wasn't there but Leonie listened to her story, and rang a friend she knew in the local police force.

'We can't do anything official unless he decides to lay charges,' the policeman told her. 'And not much unofficially without bringing abuse about police interference in citizens' lives down on our heads.'

Leonie sighed, then the man spoke again—more quietly, so that the words were inaudible to Christa. She waited patiently until the older woman hung up the phone.

'He'll run a check on the name, and also ask the hospital to let him know when they release the man. He might be able to keep tabs on him until he leaves town, but he can't promise anything.'

'All this fuss because of a "feeling" that something wasn't right,' Christa muttered apologetically.

Leonie smiled.

'Don't feel embarrassed about it,' she told her. 'I know you're a sensible, unflappable kind of person, Christa—you wouldn't make a fuss over nothing. I've taken your warning seriously and we've done what we can about it. Now, shouldn't you be at home catching up on some sleep?'

'I suppose I should.' She shifted uncomfortably on her chair, although Leonie's office was usually a haven of peace—today scented by a bowl of yellow roses on the desk. Could she talk to Leonie about Andrew?

'Everything OK?' Leonie gave her the opportunity, and Christa knew immediately that she couldn't take it. At first she'd felt that whatever was happening between her and Andrew was too new and precious to be put into words. And now? Could she reveal her own stupidity in taking the man on trust?

'Couldn't be better,' she replied with a smile that hid the turmoil within her heart.

CHAPTER TEN

BY THE time they reached the airport on Monday morning Christa was smiling again. Sam and Dawn were so excited to be going home.

They had had a great weekend and, as she'd taken her guests around the local tourist haunts and watched their wonder and amazement as they went through the tunnels of the Underwater World or rode on the cable-car that swung them to the top of the mountain behind Rainbow Bay, some of the pain had eased—although the black cloud of uncertainty still hung in her chest like an inoperable cancer.

'Happy spirits at the Bay,' Dawn said as she peered out of the window for a last look at the sparkling, sunrise-coloured water. 'They dance in the rainbows for luck and love. Rainbows joining people together, you see.'

Christa listened to the hesitant words as Dawn tried to piece together a story she'd heard in childhood. So many of the native legends had been lost, she realised, when the dialects and languages of the people died out with the elders. In her own cultural heritage the old legends could still be read in their original language, although over thousands of years both words and script had changed, but a culture with no written language relied on stories being handed down from generation to generation and 'westernisation' had broken the chain in many places.

The rising sun had turned the hard-packed gravel airstrip red by the time they dropped down at Caltura. Christa's heart beat to a frantic rhythm that was part expectation

and part dread. It was unlikely that she would see Andrew
until dinnertime—when nightfall had made further work
at the out-station impossible. Would he tell her about his
trip to Melbourne? And did she have the courage to ask
him outright if he didn't mention it?

The truck was there to meet them, and they rode the
short distance to the community hall. As always, she left
her overnight bag on the back of the truck with Jack's and
that of the pilot, Bill. Would it be left at the schoolhouse
with the others, or would word have spread and her bag
go on to the newly opened house?

She felt anticipation sizzle inside her, then remembered
that Andrew had been in town and anger swamped the
sizzle.

She worked her way through the women who were
waiting to see her—weighing and admiring babies,
injecting, suggesting, listening. A day like any other day,
but at the end of the work—what?

'I'm going to whisk your nurse away,' Andrew announced
to Jack when they had finished dinner and were sitting
talking quietly with Bill and a few of the locals who had
come to the community hall to join them for the meal.

Jack nodded absent-mindedly, and continued a dis-
cussion he was having about the use of herbal remedies.

For a moment Christa hesitated, not wanting a confron-
tation with this man who, in spite of all her attempts to
ignore his presence, had her pulses rioting.

'We've walked together often enough after dinner for
Jack not to notice our absence,' he said, as if he had sensed
her reluctance—but misread it.

He drew her away from the light of the building and
took her in his arms, holding her silently for a moment as
if to physically reassure his body that they were back

together again. She stiffened but was too weak to break the embrace.

'Am I rushing you?' he asked, sensing her withdrawal.

'No,' she said slowly, trying—not very hard—to pull away from him. His fingers were dancing down her spine, and her blood was spinning through her veins in response to the touch.

It doesn't matter why he went away, a traitorous voice whispered in her head. Pretend you don't know! Don't mention it.

'Dawn said you were in town last week.'

The words, harsher than she'd imagined they would be, came hurtling past her lips before she realised that she was about to say them.

His hands dropped away.

'I called to see her on my way through. I thought she might need money or support.'

You didn't call to see me! she wanted to yell, but she knew that she would sound like a spoiled child. Let him explain! she thought, and waited in the silent night for words that didn't come. Anxiety coiled like a snake in her stomach while her mind willed him to speak.

'She said you'd been to Melbourne!'

Christa heard the condemnation in her voice and cringed inwardly, hating herself for these petty accusations yet too disturbed by the silence and her own reactions to prevent them being said.

'I went down to see my wife—a quick, unexpected trip,' he said calmly. 'She exists, as does my son, and nothing that's said or not said between us will change that.'

Christa peered at where she knew his face was, but could see nothing in the shadows they had so deliberately sought.

'Do you still love her?'

Love her! Love her! The words seemed to echo in the

darkness, mocking Christa with their pathetic, underlying plea for a denial.

'My marriage was over a long time ago, Christa,' he said, after the echoes had nearly defeated her. 'We stayed together for appearances and, I suppose, for the sake of our son. But there's been no love between us for many years.'

He paused then added, in a deep, harsh whisper, 'No love at all!'

Somewhere above them the air moved beneath an owl's wings and, further away in the darkness, a small night creature rustled fallen leaves as it passed by on its search for food.

'So,' he said at last, 'shall I walk you home, or back to the old schoolhouse?'

She heard the desolation in his voice, and recognised it because she had felt that way herself these last few days. No love at all! she repeated to herself, and felt the elation spring back to life in her heart. The elation and the hope— and, yes, the love!

She stepped closer to him, and reached up to kiss him on the lips.

'Walk me home,' she whispered.

He responded hungrily, his arms tightening around her until she was lifted off the ground.

'Not embarrassed about what Jack or Bill might think?' he asked a little later when they drew apart to catch their breath.

She thought for a moment before she answered.

'I thought I would be,' she said at last, recognising the truth even as she spoke. 'In fact, my insides churned so much when I considered it—and other things—I thought about pleading sick and not coming.'

His arms tightened for a moment but he said nothing, so she continued in a soft, tight voice, 'But now I'm here, now that you're holding me again, I don't care if they announce it from a loudspeaker over the rooftops. I love you, Andrew Walsh,' she whispered, looking up into his face, 'and why should I be embarrassed over that?'

His head blocked out the stars as his lips met hers, gentle at first—as if drawing her commitment into his body—then heating with the drive of their physical attraction, released from the bounds of propriety and the lingering doubts that had kept them out of each other's arms for too long already.

They walked, arm in arm, towards the house, feeling the movement of each other's bodies feeding their arousal and fuelling their need for each other. And their love-making was as hot and strong and vibrant as she had imagined in her lonely bed all week, and the contentment afterwards—the warmth of body pressed to body—filled her with such joy that she wanted to laugh and cry aloud.

And waking to love? Such unimaginable pleasure, such heightened eroticism, when the mind is lulled by sleep and the body follows its own design for delight and delighting. She twisted in his arms and let him carry her to the very limits of sensation, then she moved again, learning to know his need, and heard his cry answer hers as they reached beyond the stars and found release flow through them.

'You'll miss the plane,' he whispered into her ear as she clung to him afterwards, unwilling to let even air come between them.

'I don't care,' she whispered back, and felt a thrill of shock as she realised that it was true. Suddenly there was something more important than work in her life.

But her mind regained enough control to order her body out of bed. She showered and dressed, knowing that the others would already be attacking their breakfasts. And she'd forgotten to ask Andrew the other questions she'd wanted answered. Forgotten the questions as well, she realised. Forgotten everything in the joy of being with him and in the intense satisfaction they found in each other's bodies.

She kissed him goodbye and heard him murmur something about next time, but her mind was wandering again—teasing at the thought that such delight could just be lust, not love at all.

She turned back from the doorway. He was still in bed, lying back against the pillows as if getting up and going to work was the furthest thing from his mind. He looked relaxed, and so handsome that her heart filled with pride.

He winked at her, and she smiled.

'I love you,' she said, waving her fingers in a final farewell.

'I'm glad of that,' he said, his eyes meeting and holding hers—transmitting messages she took to be a return of her love.

'Not another Base romance?' Bill said when she put in her belated appearance at the breakfast table.

'He's not staff,' she pointed out and smiled at Jack's astonishment. He was so work-focused that she would have had to make love to Andrew on the table before he noticed anything.

'No one tells me anything,' he grumbled.

'There's been nothing to tell until now,' she said, then the shadow flashed across her subconscious mind and she added honestly, 'Still nothing, really.' She could feel heat rising in her body but she stumbled on, 'It's early, exploratory stages.'

Bill chuckled and passed her a plate of toast, while Jack continued to look confused.

'Started at the wedding, didn't it?' Bill said. 'I thought there was something going on!'

'And I thought women were supposed to be the gossipy sex,' Christa chided. 'Now I suppose you'll spread it far and wide.'

'I will not,' he assured her. 'I like both you and Andrew far too much to say a word. Good luck to you both is all I say.'

'Oh, Andrew, is it?' Jack muttered, as if the only thing worrying him was the other partner in this new relationship. 'I suppose it's one way of getting a sister for his hospital.'

It couldn't be that, Christa told herself, but her heart had faltered at the words, and the bright golden glow of happiness she'd felt around her developed a tarnished appearance.

As they left the hall and walked across to the tarmac she looked around for Andrew, wanting to see him again—needing the reassurance that only his physical presence could give. He wasn't there, but she knew that his own work ethic would have hurried him out of bed as soon as she departed.

They flew on to Cameron River and another clinic, to Rosemount and another—a trip like any of the hundreds she had done in the past few years. But Jack's words lingered in her mind, and shredded her new-found confidence in love until the fortnight before she could see him again stretched ahead like an endless prison sentence.

Which ended, as fortnights always do, exactly two weeks later! This time he met the plane and took her in his arms as she reached the ground, proclaiming his love—or was it ownership?

'Cattle sales successful,' he reported, 'and I've time to

myself again. I've a week's work here sorting things out, then I'm flying south to see my son, Peter, and look at a couple of second-hand light aircraft my distribution manager's found for me. Will you put me up on my way through? Can we talk then about the future?'

He seemed so eager and excited that she chuckled and moved away from him so that she could re-examine every line of his face, checking the visual impression against the memory.

'Are you going somewhere right now that all of this can't be discussed tonight?' she asked, as her body hummed with the first tantalising thrills of anticipatory delight.

He grinned at her, and touched her lightly on the nose.

'We never seem to find time to talk at night,' he murmured.

And she remembered the shadow, and Jack's careless words, and promised soberly, 'We will tonight.'

Carla was her first patient, delighted to report that her problems had miraculously ceased.

'It's nothing miraculous and it doesn't alter the fact that you have to go to town to see a specialist,' Christa told her. She riffled through her briefcase and found the appointments she had made for Carla. 'This one's for a full blood test,' she explained, and told the girl where to find the pathology laboratory. 'I've arranged for you to go there first and then on to the specialist, a woman called Nina Jones. I've made a second tentative appointment with her a week later—by that time she'll have the test results.'

Carla nodded, seemingly resigned to the visit to town.

'I feel much better now,' she said in her soft, shy voice, 'but I wouldn't like it to start again later if I stop taking the pills—after marriage!'

She added the last words so hesitantly that Christa wondered what sex education she had received. She knew that specially trained staff conducted human relationship courses for both primary and secondary students in city schools, but thought they might be optional. And would those trained staff come this far?

As the young woman left Christa made a note on a pad to ask Nancy about it. Even in this day and age, when sexual mores were greatly relaxed, there could be a need for some premarital guidance for young people in these isolated areas.

She sighed, and wondered for a moment if things would have been different between herself and Daniel if she'd had any idea of what to expect when he first— Her mind balked at the words 'made love'. Making love was what she and Andrew did, and it bore absolutely no resemblance to the awkward, painful fumblings she'd experienced with Daniel.

Her next patient came in, then the next, and the day fell into normal rhythms until the final woman departed, shutting the door behind her. Christa remained in the room, writing notes against the names on her appointment list— who needed a follow-up appointment, who needed referral on and who should see Jack next time they came.

There was a soft rapping, then the door opened and Andrew stood there.

'I've come to take you out to dinner,' he said.

'At the little Chinese up the road?' she teased, while her body lit to flash point just looking at him.

'No, I thought we'd go French tonight,' he replied with an answering smile. 'Come on, I've already told Jack you won't be eating in the hall.'

He waited while she packed her files away and locked the door, then walked with her to the main door and out into the pale light of late afternoon.

'I've even borrowed a chariot to whisk us away,' he told her, pointing to where the old truck stood in the shade of the pepper tree.

She went with him, her body already quivering with the sexual excitement his proximity could cause. It will stop soon, this need, she assured herself, as if she'd been through it a thousand times before!

Surely it will stop soon, her less positive self pleaded.

He drove to the far side of the lagoon, where a grove of fat-trunked river gums provided shade and seclusion.

'This way,' he said as he opened the door and held out a hand to help her alight. 'It's through these trees.'

She walked with him then paused, struck again by the tranquil beauty of this shimmering stretch of water. It was red tonight, reflecting the last brilliance of the sunset, and the lily pads lay blackly on its surface, making patterns too intricate for man to copy.

Beneath a tree, above this beauty, a rug was spread and beyond it a kettle barbeque, already lit—perfuming the air with the scent of gum-leaves thrown on charcoal. Above the barbeque a lantern hung on a low branch, ready to provide light later in the evening.

'Nice spot?' Andrew asked casually and she turned to him, the wonder of it all lighting up her entire being.

She shook her head, suddenly speechless, and his eyes told her that he understood. He stepped towards her and took her in his arms, drawing her down onto the rug to lie beside him until the fire had died in the sky and the colour faded from the water.

So our bodies can lie together peacefully, she thought, contentment filling her soul with a gentle lethargy.

'Shall we eat before we kiss?' Andrew asked, and she turned to look at him, wondering if he had been thinking the same thing.

The movement was a mistake, for it brought their lips into touching distance, kissing distance—passion-building, heat-igniting, taunting, tempting kisses. Fever rose in both of them and tongues clashed, hands scrabbled with recalcitrant clothes, seeking skin and closeness and some ease from the madness that consumed them, until, urgently, ungently—in heat and haste and need—they came together, killing the pain of the long days and nights that had held them apart.

'It would have been too early to eat,' Andrew whispered after they had lain a while, spent and silent—an interval of peace while the stars broke through the dark mantle of the night sky.

Their clothes readjusted, they sat and watched the world transform itself for night, reluctant to move apart and break the spell that bound them together.

'The fire will go out before I've cooked,' he said, and Christa felt him move away, leaving a coolness on her skin. She watched him as he stirred the fire, silhouetting himself in the shower of sparks his prodding caused. Sizzling noises and the mouth-watering smell of searing meat. She stood up and walked over to stand across the fire from him, delighted by the little show of domesticity and eager to watch everything he did.

'What happened with your first wife? If your marriage was over years ago—why separate now?'

The questions were out before she'd realised it, born of seeing yet another side of this thoughtful, helpful, strong, but far from macho man.

He looked up and she could see his eyes, coal dark in the glow of the fire.

'She was willing to stay around while ever I made enough money to keep her in the style she fancied, but you must remember she married a white man. When I found out about my antecedents and began my search into the past, she couldn't understand it. Couldn't understand why anyone would want to find, let alone claim, his Aboriginality.' He looked away from her, prodding at the meat. 'For a while she went along with it, then said I had to choose.'

'Choose what?' Christa whispered, although the cold, hard voice he was using frightened her.

'Choose to keep quiet about it, keep it a secret even from my son, or she would leave me. It seems the bargain we had made to stay together was dependent on my being white!'

He flung the steaks over and added foil packets of what must be vegetables, but Christa doubted they would be eaten. Her appetite was gone, gone with the pain she could hear in Andrew's voice—with the agony she knew could only stem from love. Was it love for his son or for the woman he'd denied loving?

'I thought, for a while, I could forget my heritage but once I'd visited Caltura I knew it was impossible. It was as if my feet became rooted in the ground here so that, wherever I was, I felt it drawing me back.'

Another prod, a careless flip and the vegetable packages turned over.

'I considered what I would be leaving as a legacy for my son—money earned with long hard hours in an air-conditioned office, wheeling and dealing and making more and more until the money became the goal, not satisfaction or producing something that could be held or shown with pride and said of, "I did this".'

Christa moved closer. She slipped her arms around his waist and rested her head on his back, offering silent comfort and seeking a little solace for herself.

He's never said he loved you, she reminded herself,

trying to soothe her own devastation.

She felt him stiffen and moved away from him, aware that he'd thrown off whatever torment his memories had awoken.

'We'd better eat,' he said, his voice as remote as the moon that was straining its light through the leaves on the trees above them.

He produced plates and cutlery, condiments, glasses and wine from a cardboard box at the base of another tree, and served up a simple but delicious meal. Christa forced herself to eat, although her own unhappiness seemed to have formed itself into a lump that was lodged in her throat.

They talked about the cattle sales; about the new breeding stock the money would buy; about the satellite dish he'd ordered to connect Caltura to the cellular phone network, and how much easier his life would be once he had a light aircraft.

Easier to get to Melbourne; easier to see the woman you say you don't love!

'You're tired,' he said at last, as if suddenly realising that her responses lacked the correct amount of enthusiasm. 'Let's go home to bed. We'll have time to talk again in the morning.'

Will we? Christa wondered, but she helped him pack away the picnic things and, with a last, regretful look at the lagoon—magical in the moonlight—she followed him to the 'chariot'.

'I'll clean up the mess while you have a shower,' he said when they reached the house. His voice was deep with concern—for her, she knew! He was assuming that her quietness stemmed from tiredness, and probably castigating himself for keeping her out late. At other times this thoughtfulness of his was like a security blanket, but tonight it irritated her.

'I'll help with the dishes,' she said. 'It's not late.'

He put down the box at the top of the steps and turned towards her.

'I know it's not late,' he murmured, and touched her hair, her cheek and then her lips.

The tremors began again, even before he moved closer and kissed her long and hard—not holding her, their lips the only parts of their bodies in contact.

'Perhaps we'll leave the dishes and both have a shower.'

He raised his head enough to look into her face, and the desire that shone like shards of silver in his eyes shot through her like a lightning bolt.

Yet, even as his hands soaped her body—finding secret places to inflame with hunger for him—the shadow grew and grew in her mind until pure, rippling waves of sensation washed away all thought.

They had just emerged from the shower, and Andrew was towelling her dry, when they heard the call from outside.

'Jack says can you come, Sister?'

Christa pulled on her dirty clothes, and pushed her damp feet into her sandals. She brushed her fingers through her hair to push it back from her face, and hurried outside.

'I'll drive you—it's quicker than walking,' Andrew said, and she realised that he'd been dressing at the same time.

Lights shone from the hospital windows, and an anxious crowd was gathered at the foot of the steps.

'Helen's baby come,' someone whispered as they drew near.

Jack met her in the ward.

'She's in the theatre; Nellie's with her. Did you see her earlier today?' he asked.

'No, she didn't come last clinic either and I assumed she'd gone to Castleford—she must be thirty-six weeks.'

'And the rest, I'd say. I think she decided to have the baby here whatever happened, and has been fudging her dates.'

'I should have realised that when I examined her,' Christa said. 'Shall I go on in and see her?'

'In a minute,' Jack replied. 'She's doing fine—contractions about two minutes apart. As far as I can tell everything's normal.'

'As far as you can tell?' Christa repeated incredulously.

'I've only talked to her, not examined her. It seems this is women's business,' he said, shrugging and smiling at the same time. 'They want you in there, not me.'

Christa shook her head, but she also smiled.

'And how many women are going to be giving me advice?' she asked.

'Only Nellie and Nancy. I sent the rest out.' He paused, looking thoughtful, then continued, 'When you get talking, see if you can find out if she took something to bring on the labour. It seems too coincidental to me—this baby arriving while we are here.'

Christa considered this for a moment.

'Well, I know they have berries and plants they can eat that help contraception, so why not something to promote labour? What about anaesthetic? Did you talk to her about a painkiller?'

'I don't think that will be necessary either,' Jack said slowly. 'She's so cheerful you'd swear she was on her way to a party. Even when the contractions are strongest she just smiles.'

'I'd better go in and check on things,' Christa said, but Jack was miles away.

'So much natural medicine has been lost because we didn't value it—because we arrogantly assumed our medicine would be superior,' he fretted, and Christa patted him on the arm.

'Go and talk to Andrew about it. He might be able to persuade the elders to write down what they know. In the meantime, I'll get on with the "women's business".'

She left him and walked through to the store-room for clean linen and one of the 'baby-bundles' that had been bought in anticipation of such an event.

'Here's our own sister,' Nancy greeted her when she entered the small theatre.

Jack had been right—a party atmosphere pervaded the place. Helen was sitting on the edge of the operating table, swinging her legs and every few minutes hunching over to ease the pain.

'She's been walking round, but I told her to sit a while,' Nellie announced, and Christa wondered how the forebears of these women had had their children. Had they lain down—or squatted, as some women seemed to prefer?

She pulled on a gown, scrubbed and drew on gloves, then, as Helen lay back against pillows Nancy had stacked behind her, Christa checked the foetal pulse and dilation of the cervix.

'Everything fine, see,' Nellie said, and Christa smiled at the incongruous sight of the big woman with a gown pulled over her floral nightdress and latex gloves white against her dark skin.

Nancy was standing by Helen's head, wiping her forehead with a damp cloth and talking softly in their own language.

'Now you're coming we might arrange a room better

than this for births,' Nellie suggested and Christa looked at her, puzzled by the assumption.

'When you marry Andrew and come to be our nurse,' Nellie explained, then chuckled, before she added, 'Good thing Nancy adopt you, not me. If I adopt you then you can't marry Andrew because you'd be cousins, and there'd still be no nurse.'

She laughed uproariously as if this would be the greatest joke, but it was the second time today that a conversation had prodded Christa's uncertainty back to life.

Then the moment was lost as the tempo in the room quickened, and Helen cried out with a need to push. Christa moved to her side, checking blood pressure, pulse and tiny heartbeat once again—forgetting her doubts about Andrew and his plans in the adrenalin rush that always accompanied her participation in a baby's birth.

'Let Nellie—you watch!' Helen gasped, and Christa stood aside. She had an injection drawn up to help contract Helen's uterus after the birth, but it would stay where it was until she was convinced that the young woman wanted it. It seemed as if there were other forces—possibly other drugs—at work here. Perhaps Nellie's knowledge was every bit as effective as hers!

'See, I do it all easily,' Nellie told her later and Christa realised, as she held the tiny, well-wrapped infant against her breast while Nancy sponged Helen and helped her into a nightdress, that Nellie had, indeed, done it all.

'If there'd been a complication would you have managed?' she asked.

'I've done bottom-first and even feet-first, turning them with my hand,' Nellie explained. 'Only one dead baby in forty, fifty maybe, and he was dead before the mother started having pains. No kicking and she was so sick, we knew.'

The woman spoke with such certainty that Christa asked, 'Did you have some training when you were young?'

'Only what my mother taught me—and her mother, and her mother,' Nellie said, and a tiny spurt of excitement shifted in Christa's stomach. She could understand what Jack meant about natural drugs and remedies being lost. This birth had been as relaxed and pain-controlled as any she had ever witnessed and, as she'd suspected, Helen had rejected her drug in favour of a cup of brewed tea Nellie had ready for her.

A new excitement sprang to life within Christa. If she came to live at Caltura would Nellie eventually share her secrets? Could she, perhaps, find out more about the medicine of these ancient people, and use her knowledge to help others in the world beyond Caltura's boundaries?

If she came to Caltura. . .

'Can we see Mick now?' Helen asked and Nellie, the self-appointed boss, nodded and led the new mother, proudly holding her baby, through to the ward. Nancy called to Mick, then she and Christa walked out onto the verandah and down the steps.

'Everything OK?' Jack asked, extracting himself from the group of people beneath a tree in what had once been the school playground.

'Fine,' she assured him. 'A baby boy they are going to call Jack—because you didn't deliver him.'

'I went through far more agony out here,' Jack told her. 'Now I know how expectant fathers feel. Should I check him?'

'Later, when he's met his own father,' Christa suggested, 'but he's fine. I did an Apgar and a thorough examination, and took blood for a PKU. I think your big decision is going to be what next?'

'What next?' Jack echoed. 'Oh, you mean, do we take them both back to town or leave them here?'

'Exactly!' Christa said. 'Although you might not have a choice. I'd say they've decided to stay, and Nellie has taken over my job completely. She'll sleep at the hospital with Helen, and probably Mick and various others, until she judges they're both right to go home.'

'Well, it's no different from a home birth, I suppose,' Jack remarked. 'And if Nellie's in charge, you'd better get some sleep—we've the double clinic tomorrow.'

Another figure split from the group and moved towards her.

'I'll take her home,' Andrew said to Jack and then, as he led her away with his arm around her shoulders, he whispered teasingly, 'Though I don't know if sleep was what you had in mind, Sister Cassimatis.'

'It's not,' she said abruptly, and felt his arm stiffen against her in reaction to the terseness in her voice.

Not wanting to make a scene in front of the others, she waited until they were in the truck—until he'd started the engine and was driving away.

'It's all been part of the grand plan, hasn't it?'

The words stormed from her lips but he held up his hand, silencing her.

'Let's wait until we get to the house and can sit and look at each other, Christa,' he said, and she noticed that he hadn't used the word 'home' a second time.

Gritting her teeth to keep a rein on her tongue, she waited, but the fury built inside her—coming like a black tide out of nowhere and sweeping through the desolation of her soul.

'It's an arranged marriage, isn't it? That's what this whole seduction has been about!' She hurled the words towards the darker darkness that was his figure in the night-gloom of the house. 'Only this was arranged by you, instead of my parents. A marriage of convenience, so you could get a nurse for your precious hospital sooner than the five years it would take for one of the local people to train!'

'I never pretended it was anything else,' he said gravely, fuelling her rage. 'I thought you understood that because arranged marriages are as much part of your heritage as they are of mine.'

'They are a part of my heritage I left home to escape,' she yelled. 'I told you that! I told you that's why I took up nursing.'

'And I told you we should explore what was between us and see what we could make of what we have got, not what we haven't.'

The statement, so calm and restrained, was bleak enough to chill her anger for a moment.

'But you were so. . .so manipulative about it!' She wished that she could see his face—wished that she could claw at it and hit him, her disappointment was so acute. 'I was so excited when Nancy "adopted" me—so pleased and proud. And now I see your hand behind it—organising it so I can be acceptable to the community—even arranging for me to be adopted into a family that's on your "marriage" list!'

She paused, pain swamping her anger.

'I had nothing to do with your "adoption",' he said, too calmly. 'Marrying me would have brought you into my family—you would have been acceptable.'

'Well, I'm pleased about that!' she snapped, not knowing whether his explanation made things better or worse. The 'would have' hammered in her heart—slotting whatever they did have into the past.

'You were pleased about other things,' he reminded her,

stepping closer so that she could feel his body heat and hear him breathing. 'You must admit that what we do have adds up to something special, Christa.'

His voice was husky and familiar. So familiar from seduction that it scorched along her nerves.

She stepped away from him, distancing herself—not willing to be seduced again—and drawing desperately on her reserves of strength to finish what she had started.

'What we have is sex,' she said bluntly, and even in the darkness she saw him stiffen.

'Not friendship?' he asked in a hard, cold voice. 'Not companionship and mutual respect; not the ability to laugh together? Has there been none of that for you? Just sex?'

She knew that she'd lost him, and in that instant she also knew that she loved him. True, she'd said the words before, but lightly—in the grip of new and wondrous feelings—not like this kind of knowing, when the revelation brought despair and agony along with it.

CHAPTER ELEVEN

'You want love? False declarations that will make our lives together more palatable? Our sexual acts more acceptable?'

Andrew's voice rasped across the room, but before Christa could lie and deny it he was speaking again.

'And what is love?' he asked. 'I'll tell you what it is, Christa. It's a four-letter word, that's all. It's not some secret talisman that will shield you from pain and grief and loneliness; it's not some magic potion that will make one marriage work while others disintegrate into bitterness and hatred. I tried love once,' he said grimly. 'I believed it made the world go round, moved mountains and swung on stars—but it's an illusion, a joke! Love's a word, Christa, that's all it is but, even to have you as my wife, I won't lie and say it.'

Her body felt as if it were icing up, while her head knew that he was speaking the truth—or his perspective of it! Yet love existed, she knew that. It was her inexperience that made it hard to find a definition she could use to refute his words.

He crossed the room and took her gently in his arms, rubbing his hands up and down her back to bring warmth back to her skin and bones. She wondered if his anger could dissipate so suddenly, then felt his control in rigid muscles and heard the tension in his voice.

'Come to bed; you're cold,' he murmured. 'I won't stay if you don't want me. We began as friends, Christa. Can't we at least salvage that from this mess? Can't we hold onto that at the moment, and leave the future to itself for a while?'

She allowed him to lead her into the bedroom and she fell into bed, shivering now in the aftermath of her emotional storm. He drew the covers up around her then, as her trembling continued, he cursed silently and slid into bed beside her, warming her against his body and soothing her until she drifted off to sleep.

She woke to sunlight filtering through the trees beyond the windows, and her body betraying her decision to be finished with this man.

'Love does exist,' she said aloud, hoping that confirmation of her thoughts would bring her physical self back into line!

'Of course it does, in many guises,' he agreed—too easily. 'It's a word we use to describe our feelings for our parents, our children, our friends—and sometimes a painting, or a beautiful view, or chocolate cake—but it's still a word, Christa, and only a word.'

He had trivialised it with the chocolate cake and she shifted away from him, her body finally subdued. She pushed herself out of bed and turned to face him, dirty and dishevelled.

'I could go along with all your arguments if I thought you believed that,' she said, looking down at his dark, unshaven face. 'But love did exist for you. I heard it in your voice when you spoke of your wife; I heard the pain it can cause people, grating from your heart. You're denying it now because you're either frightened of it or carrying it entombed for her.'

She paused and felt the morning sun touch her arm, like a spirit message sent to strengthen her. She lifted her head and continued, her voice calm and controlled.

'I love you, Andrew, probably enough to marry you

without your loving me—to marry you for your convenience. But arranged marriages in my culture are made
in the belief that love will grow between the two people,
and that's not possible where one of those involved isn't
willing to give love a chance—by simply denying its
existence.'

She walked out of the room, picked up her overnight
bag and went straight out of the house. She would have
a shower and change at the hospital and people could think
what they liked.

One look at her face at breakfast must have warned her
two colleagues to say nothing, so Helen's baby was discussed and then talk turned to Cameron River and
Rosemount—the two visits on their list for today. Andrew
made no appearance at the airfield, nor did he come to
town the following weekend—the weekend he'd intended
discussing marriage plans!

Christa moved through the days with a mechanical
efficiency, her smile so false that it made her cheeks ache.
At night she lay awake, Wally—allowed inside to sleep
in an attempt to ease her loneliness—snuggled at the end
of the bed. She had days off and more on duty. Days
dragged by in a blur of activity. She was on call, but
working in the office, three weeks later when the late-
afternoon message came through from Wollombi, a
fly-speck of a town south of Ruthven. It was garbled but
the general gist of it was, 'Get here quick'.

Eddie met her at the airport, and they left together. Nick
was back from his honeymoon but off duty, while Peter
and Jack were both on clinics.

By the time they arrived, landing on a road that ran by
the river, the policeman from Ruthven had reached the
scene—a camp-site beneath the river-gums not far from

the pub that was Wollombi. Before she saw the bodies
Christa knew the cause.

'John Gordon!' she whispered, and took hold of
Eddie's hand.

'We don't need a woman here,' the policeman yelled
at Eddie but she walked on with him, trembling fingers
clutching the equipment bag and her hammering heart
preparing her for the worst.

'I'm a nurse,' she stammered at him, although she was
almost certain that she had come too late.

The redness of the bare earth was repeated on the chests
of the victims. Blood soaked through sleeping bags and
piles of clothes, and fed the ants that were already crawl-
ing closer.

She let her clinical self take over, knowing that surgery
she'd seen had looked far worse. She knelt by one, by
two inert bodies before she found a pulse in the third. The
girl was breathing—shallowly, but on her own. Christa
slipped a mask over the white face, covering the mouth
and nose, and attached it to oxygen.

'Leave the stretcher, Eddie, and get the Thomas pack,'
she said, opening her case for wadding to stuff into the
wound and a sling to use as a tourniquet to shut off blood
supply to an arm that would have to be amputated. Her
eyes catalogued the signs of massive blood loss and shock.
She tried to remember recent studies on the use of fluids
where haemorrhage had occurred—blood products, not
fluids, she remembered—and fed a tube into the young
girl's uninjured arm.

'The MAST trousers,' she said to Eddie when he
returned. 'Let's see if they will help.'

He pulled them from the pack while she attached the
monitor to the girl, then directed him while he fastened
them around the girl's legs and pelvis then inflated them.

'Not too much,' she warned him. 'We want her on the plane as soon as possible, and I'll have to reduce the pressure as we climb.'

There was a cry in the distance, and the policeman hurried away.

Concentrate on the girl, she told herself. Don't think of how it happened, or why—your job is to keep her alive.

With Eddie's help, she lifted her patient onto the stretcher.

'Will you take the others now?' the policeman said to Eddie, and Christa shuddered. She'd flown with bodies before—it was part of the job. But she couldn't bear to see them loaded on like nothings—life drained away by someone's madness.

'I'll come back,' Eddie said, as if he'd read her thoughts. 'You'll be a while, taking photographs and such. We'll see what we can do for the living.'

They flew out soon afterwards, Christa so intent on her patient that she was unaware of time passing. She had begun to believe that she was winning when the girl's blood pressure began to rise, but when the plane touched down at the Bay she greeted the paramedic who had accompanied the ambulance with a glad sigh of relief.

'There's a policeman to see you, Christa,' Eddie said as the ambulance drove away. 'I'm taking him back out to Wollombi. He'd like you to come with us—seems to think you know something about all of this.'

Eddie sounded both annoyed and protective, and he frowned when she said, 'I'll come,' and followed him back onto the plane.

He was obviously trying to shield her from any further trauma, but she'd seen the shotgun pellets that had caused the wounds. A gun had been held close to the victims' chests, tearing gaping wounds in lungs and heart and tissues. The girl they'd brought back to town must have been sleeping on her side for her arm had taken the worst of the shot.

And the last time she'd seen shotgun pellets they had been in John Gordon's arm.

Three policemen, loaded down with equipment, clambered on board, one introducing himself as Len Stephens, the friend Leonie had contacted when Christa had blurted out her concern about the strange patient she'd brought to town.

'We tried to keep an eye on him,' he explained to Christa as the men pushed their bags under their seats and strapped in for take-off. 'We notified all the local flight offices to watch out for him and warned the mail pilot he might be looking for a lift, but we thought he was safe in hospital for a while—and we weren't told when he checked himself out.'

'If it was him, he managed to get out there somehow,' Christa said as the futility of it all began to eat into her heart. 'And where is he now—when the damage is done?' she asked bitterly.

'He could have gone south and a chartered a plane to take him to Ruthven, or hired a car and driven out there,' Mike explained, adding, 'We think we have found him although, as you say, it's too late!'

His voice was gentle and he continued talking, as if he understood her need to know. 'The other girl raised the alarm. Seems she'd been feeling sick the previous night and had gone into town and stayed at the pub. She returned early in the morning, saw her friends and raced back to tell someone. I had word from the Ruthven policeman that they've found a third male body some distance away with a shotgun lying beside it. That accounts for them all, I think.'

She should have been pleased, or relieved, but the waste

of life was too shocking for her to feel anything more than added regret.

'Why didn't they wake up?' Christa asked. 'Shotguns have to be loaded. Wouldn't the others have woken at the first shot and tried to get away, or tried to stop him?'

'I haven't seen them yet,' Mike reminded her, 'but the likelihood is they were drugged. The hospital reported a small package of drugs missing some days after he left. They were narcotics but only mild ones, so not kept in the secure cupboard. No one thought to connect a single patient's departure with the theft—or not up until now!'

She let it all sink in, while the one question that hadn't been answered fluttered on her lips.

At last she asked.

'Why?'

'They call it love,' the policeman said bitterly. 'Seems he loved the girl you saved, but she wanted one of the other fellows.' He sighed. 'Or both of them—who knows? What she didn't want were the attentions of John Gordon, and so he killed them all.'

Love!

Perhaps Andrew had been right—it was just a word with misused, over-emphasised powers!

Love—and Andrew—and senseless death—and choc- olate cake! Her throat filled with tears but she held them back.

If love didn't exist, could sorrow?

Back at the site she identified the body of the man she'd met as John Gordon, then returned to the plane and moved to the front. She would sit in the copilot's seat and stay there until everyone came on board, had been flown back to the Bay and had left the plane again. Then—if her legs and arms were obeying her brain—she would walk to her car, drive herself home, crawl into bed and pull the covers over her head—possibly for a fortnight.

Resolutely ignoring all the activity around her, she closed her eyes and waited—feeling motion, flight, wheels thumping back to earth—refusing even to think!

Jack and Leonie were waiting when she finally decided that she could face the world again and emerged from her hunched position in the cockpit.

'Come to my place,' Leonie urged, but Christa shook her head.

'I want to go home!' she muttered. 'Home!'

They drove her home and Jack fed her brandy although she wasn't certain that was medicinally correct for shock, which she assumed she was suffering.

'I'll stay with her,' she heard Leonie say.

'I'll be all right,' she said, but her voice seemed to be coming from a long way off. 'I'll have a shower,' she added, thinking that a show of normality might send them on their way. 'Then go to bed.'

'We'll stay here until you come out,' Leonie promised.

Too weary to argue any more, she headed for the bathroom. Wally whimpered from the bed, but she didn't have the strength to reassure him. Energy was draining from her like the sawdust stuffing from a toy. She showered and washed her hair, but felt the lingering stickiness of blood on her hands like an invisible curse.

Leonie took her soiled clothes away, and helped her into a warm nightgown.

'Please go; I'll be all right,' she begged Leonie, knowing that tears were close but not wanting to cry with the other woman watching her. Not wanting to cry at all in case she might never stop.

'OK,' Leonie said and leant towards her, giving her a soft kiss on the cheek.

Then Jack was there, touching her wrist, helping her

into bed and drawing the covers over her.

'It's two now,' he murmured, his voice deep with concern. 'Leonie and I will go, but I'll be back at six in the morning to see that you're all right. In the meantime, ring if you get lonely or if the shivering starts again.'

She hadn't known that she'd been shivering but, when she'd heard the door shut and knew that they had gone, she felt the bed begin to shake.

This is what you wanted, she reminded herself when sleep wouldn't come, and she had to open her eyes to keep the nightmare images from recurring. You wanted to come home and crawl into bed.

She looked out of the window, seeking trees with leaves silvered by the moon, and saw only the eaves of Bobbie's house next door.

This wasn't home, her spirit whispered, and now she closed her eyes and let the grief flow out in tears.

The spasm finally ended and she got out of bed, pulled on her robe and headed for the kitchen. She made a pot of tea, keeping busy so that she didn't have to think about that sudden revelation, but when it was brewed she poured a cup and carried it out to the verandah. She sat on the top step, Wally cuddled up beside her, and looked up at the stars.

Love and destruction!

She'd witnessed that destructive force last night but, prior to that, she'd let that simple, four-letter word destroy the best thing that had ever happened to her—let it tear her apart from a man whose worth could not be measured or quantified by words.

She breathed deeply, tasting the salt in the air but missing the bite of the eucalypts. Could she go back? Turn time around? What bits of the present would have been changed if she'd not demanded 'love' from Andrew? Her course would have been altered, but would the course of others' lives—of the young people who were killed so senselessly at a lonely campsite?

And would Andrew have her back? Would he believe that she had accepted his terms and would not ask for more than he could give?

She sought answers from the stars, but none came. Instead, there was peace of a kind—a quiet acceptance, although parts of her still cried out—and guilt that she had not done more to save those souls still beat beneath her ribs.

A noise shattered the silence of the early-morning hours and she wrapped her arms around her body, shocked by the anger this disruption caused. As it came closer she recognised the roar of a motorbike—not muffled in any way—disrupting her fragile peace and hammering against her ears.

She closed her eyes and drew back into the shadows, hoping to hide from its raucous insistence. Then it stopped, and the silence intensified.

It had stopped close by, she realised, peering out of the shadows—frightened now, aware that she would be exposed if the ghostly rider came towards her house, not some other.

John Gordon's dead, she reminded herself as the panic escalated into heart-jolting hysteria. Then Wally moved, whimpering a welcome and wiggling down the steps, belly ingratiatingly lowered to the ground.

'Hush, Wally, don't wake her,' a voice whispered, a clear voice that was full of musical tones.

'I'm not asleep,' she whispered, and leaned forward from her hiding-place, then heard his cry and saw him take the steps in two bounds to crouch beside her and pull her into his arms.

'Oh, Christa! Are you OK, my darling?' he murmured against her hair. 'Such horror, such tragedy for you to witness! Jack radioed to tell me you'd been called to the scene as soon as he heard. I imagined your pain, your devastation at such senseless killing, and knew I had to get to you.' He kissed her ear, then added, 'But it's a damn long way on an unreliable bloody bike.'

She'd never heard him swear before, she thought, rubbing her cheek against his face and feeling the roughness of dust. He'd ridden through the night to be with her, to hold her close—exactly as he'd known she needed to be held.

Her arms crept around his body and his tightened, rocking her against him as if he would never let her go.

'I was wrong about love,' he said hoarsely. 'It's more than a word.'

She couldn't speak as her throat was too full of tears, and as she waited he spoke again.

'It's so many things—I know that now. It's the ache of emptiness when you're not in bed with me, the silly smile that used to creep across my lips on Monday mornings when your plane was due in. It's feeling complete when you're around—even if you're not right by my side—and feeling only half a person when you're not there. It's the bitter pain I felt, knowing I had hurt you, and the despair that tore me apart when I knew you needed me—and I wasn't there for you. It's happiness, and wholeness, and the future, and—for me—it's you, my love.'

She felt the words, like rose-petals, fall about her and sat, motionless, knowing that it must all be a dream and fearing that the slightest movement might wake her. Then she'd lose the dream, and Andrew with it.

'It's not too late?' he asked, his voice loud enough to

break the dream. She moved and found that his body remained in place, solid and warm against hers.

'Too late?' she repeated, her mind bamboozled by dreams—and now battling to cope with reality in the form of cryptic questions.

'Too late for you and me? Too late to say I love you, Christa, and mean it with all my heart and soul?'

I love you, Christa! The words rattled in her ears and echoed through the void that was her brain.

'You said you wouldn't say that for the sake of it,' she reminded him, miraculously recovering the power of speech now that something so important needed to be straightened out.

'And I meant it,' he whispered, 'which is why I'll say it now. I love you, Christa.'

He kissed her on the lips, a confirmation of the pledge, and she tasted dirt and grit.

Other things fell into place.

'You rode here? On one of those old bikes?' she asked, incredulously considering the tortuous road and his six- or seven-hour ride.

'How else was I to come? No plane as yet. I seemed to lose interest in other projects for a while back there.'

There was a rueful quality about the words, but a tiredness as well.

'You must be exhausted,' she scolded, as her mind began to work again. 'And here we are sitting on the verandah like two homeless waifs. Come inside and have a shower. I'll get you tea and something to eat.'

His head bent and dusty lips brushed across her temple.

'I came to look after you, my darling, not the other way around.'

'Come inside anyway,' she suggested, weakened by the magnitude of his decision.

They stood, still holding tightly to each other, and she led him into the house and turned on the light.

He was covered in dust, a grey-brown coating that fell about him as he moved. His face was rimed with dirt where his helmet had been, and his hair was pressed flat and held in place by sweat.

Eyes, red-rimmed with fatigue, peered out at her and he held out his hands, as if presenting himself for inspection, and shrugged.

She looked at him for a moment, seeing the dark lines of strain in his face and the uncertainty that lingered in his hesitant stance—yet the silver glitter in his eyes confirmed for her that love existed.

And she knew that the destructive force she'd witnessed earlier had nothing to do with love.

'You do still believe in love?' he asked, tentative for such a positive man.

'Of course,' she replied, and smiled, because she even knew, now, what it looked like.

MILLS & BOON®

Medical Romance™

COMING NEXT MONTH

THE PERFECT WIFE AND MOTHER?
by Caroline Anderson
Audley Memorial Hospital

Ryan O'Connor wanted a lover. No commitment, no ties. And Ginny Jeffries agreed, against her better judgement, to accept Ryan O'Connor's terms. But being his lover meant deepening ties with Ryan and his two small children, and all she could see ahead was heartbreak...

INTIMATE PRESCRIPTION by Margaret Barker

Adam Lennox was surprised to see that Trisha Redman was a mother. Eight years previously she had refused to marry him because she was fearful of a physical relationship. So how could she enjoy a physical relationship with another man? Would Trisha tell Adam the truth?

PROMISE OF A MIRACLE by Marion Lennox
Gundowring Hospital

Meg Preston's quiet visit to Gundowring took an unexpected turn when she fell into the path—and home—of Rob Daniels. Before she knew it she was bound up in the Gundowring way of life and was falling in love with Rob! But Meg had a fiancé waiting in England...

WINNING THROUGH by Laura MacDonald

Dr Harry Brolin forecast that Kirstin Patterson would only survive one month as a GP in his tough inner city practice. She soon proved that she could handle even the most perilous of situations. But could she handle her dangerous feelings for Harry?

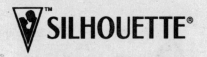

▼™ SILHOUETTE®

Tempting...Tantalising...Terrifying!

Strangers
in the night

Three spooky love stories in one compelling
volume by three masters of the genre:

Dark Journey by Anne Stuart
Catching Dreams by Chelsea Quinn Yarbro
Beyond Twilight by Maggie Shayne

Available: July 1997   Price: £4.99

SUMMER SEARCH

How would you like to win a year's supply of Mills & Boon® books? Well you can and they're FREE! Simply complete the competition below and send it to us by 31st December 1997. The first five correct entries picked after the closing date will each win a year's subscription to the Mills & Boon series of their choice. What could be easier?

SPADE
SUNSHINE
PICNIC
BEACHBALL
SWIMMING
SUNBATHING
CLOUDLESS
FUN
TOWEL
SAND
HOLIDAY

W	Q	T	U	H	S	P	A	D	E	M	B
E	Q	R	U	O	T	T	K	I	U	I	E
N	B	G	H	L	H	G	O	D	W	K	A
I	I	O	A	I	N	E	S	W	Q	L	C
H	N	U	N	D	D	F	W	P	E	O	H
S	U	N	B	A	T	H	I	N	G	L	B
N	S	E	A	Y	F	C	M	D	A	R	A
U	B	P	K	A	N	D	M	N	U	T	L
S	E	N	L	I	Y	B	I	A	N	U	L
H	B	U	C	K	E	T	N	S	N	U	E
T	A	E	W	T	O	H	G	H	O	T	F
C	L	O	U	D	L	E	S	S	P	W	N

C7F

Please turn over for details of how to enter ☞

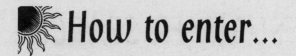# How to enter...

Hidden in the grid are eleven different summer related words. You'll find the list beside the word puzzle overleaf and they can be read backwards, forwards, up, down and diagonally. As you find each word, circle it or put a line through it. When you have found all eleven, don't forget to fill in your name and address in the space provided below and pop this page in an envelope (you don't even need a stamp) and post it today. Hurry competition ends 31st December 1997.

Mills & Boon Summer Search Competition
FREEPOST, Croydon, Surrey, CR9 3WZ
EIRE readers send competition to PO Box 4546, Dublin 24.

Please tick the series you would like to receive if you are a winner
Presents™ ❑   Enchanted™ ❑   Temptation® ❑
Medical Romance™ ❑   Historical Romance™ ❑

Are you a Reader Service™ Subscriber?   Yes ❑   No ❑

Ms/Mrs/Miss/Mr _____
                                                            (BLOCK CAPS PLEASE)
Address _____

_____

_____ Postcode _____

(I am over 18 years of age)